New Directions in Prose and Poetry 40

Edited by J. Laughlin

with Peter Glassgold and Frederick R. Martin

 A New Directions Book

ACKNOWLEDGMENTS
Grateful acknowledgment is made to the editors and publishers of books and magazines in which some of the selections in this volume first appeared: for John Allman, *Specialia: Contemporary America Poetry* and *Sunbury* (Copyright © 1976 by John Allman); for Doug Crowell, *Fiction Texas* (Copyright © 1978 by Fiction Texas); for Lawrence Ferlinghetti, *San Francisco Examiner* (Copyright © 1979 by Lawrence Ferlinghetti); for David Giannini, *Longhouse* (Copyright © 1978 by David Giannini); for Jerome Rothenberg, *River Styx* (Copyright © 1975 by Jerome Rothenberg) and *Out of the West*.

Jean Cocteau's "The Crucifixion" (*"La Crucifixion"*), included in *Poemes* (© Editions Gallimard 1948), appears by permission of Editions Gallimard, Paris.

William Heinesen's "The Night of the Gryla" originates from the volume *Det Fortryellede lys* (*"The Enchanted Light"*), © 1957 by William Heinesen, and appears in translation by permission of the publisher, Gyldendal, Copenhagen.

James Purdy's "Clearing in the Forest," Copyright © 1978 by James Purdy.

Manufactured in the United States of America
First published clothbound (ISBN: 0-8112-0762-5) and as New Directions Paperbook 500 (ISBN: 0-8112-0763-3) in 1980
Published simultaneously in Canada by George J. McLeod, Ltd., Toronto

New Directions Books are published for James Laughlin
by New Directions Publishing Corporation,
80 Eighth Avenue, New York 10011

CONTENTS·

THE WHITE NEWSY

LAWRENCE FERLINGHETTI

The old newsy in the old porkpie hat
is taking his coffee-break
He has his doughnut broken in pieces
spread out on his napkin
He has a red poppy in his hat
a Memorial Day poppy
American Legion poppy
It's the week of Memorial Day
the week after ex-cop White got off
for killing Milk and Moscone
The newsy is reading his paper
It's serious business reading the paper
He has it folded over
but not the New York subway-fold
No he's a San Franciscan
an old-line San Franciscan
born South of the Slot
whose grandfather came over
during the Great Potato Famine
and his father a Muni conductor
reading his son what Yeats wrote
about the Irish Rebellion
The kid went to work selling papers

not too far from City Hall
He hawked headlines shrill and clear
He hawked SACCO & VANZETTI TO DIE!
           LAST APPEAL FAILS!
He hawked F.D.R. ASSASSINATION ATTEMPT!
           MAYOR OF CHICAGO SHOT DEAD!
He hawked ASSASSIN GETS CHAIR!
He holds the paper close up and scans it
He has thick rimless eyeglasses
He's reading the Great Whitewash
He takes a swig of coffee
without taking his eyes from the white page
What's happening to this town?
Everything is backwards
Mere anarchy is loosed
Do anything and get away with it
Free all felons for crimes of passion
Free all political prisoners
He squints at the paper
Maybe it's his eyes
They kept him out of the service
so he just went on hawking headlines
J.F.K. ASSASSINATED!
BOBBY DIES!
MOSCONE & MILK DEAD!
All the truth that's fit to print
All his life he's been serving up the truth
All these years he's been buying the poppy
He liked to see the big shots and the hot shots
coming and going at City Hall
He admired their limousines and the police escorts
He admired the white cops in their blue uniforms
Now he keeps turning the paper
He sees red not white
The hand that pulled the trigger felled a city!
He reads how the triggerman got off
He reads how there's two standards of justice—
one for the White and one for the rest of the world
He reads how Law and Order must prevail

over 'our ungovernable rage for justice'
He reads how the jury decided one life
is not worth more than another
He reads about the Milk of Human Kindness
He reads how the jury saw white on white
He reads how they saw a good person
from good people
with a good background
a good man with a gun
He reads how the jury made history
how the jury made a great leap forward
to a new higher level of consciousness
Out here we're still the first frontier
No more an eye for an eye
nor a tooth for a tooth
No more of that barbarity
He bites the last of his doughnut
He gulps the last of his coffee
His head is heavy under the poppy
He gets himself together and heads out
There's cops riding by in a squad car
their siren singing
Suddenly the newsy starts shouting
and waving his papers
All the headlines he's ever hawked
come back to him
He doesn't seem to know what he's shouting
He must be crazy
He's making up his own reality
NO MORE CRIME & PUNISHMENT!
NO MORE SWIFT RETRIBUTION!
NO MORE GUNS & BOMBS!
REJOICE IN THE LAMB
AND THE LION AND LAMB
SHALL LIE TOGETHER!
SWEEP UP THE GLASS! UNBOARD THE GREAT WINDOWS!

STANDARD—12,
YOU STEPPED OUT OF A DREAM
(OF POWER)

TOBY OLSON

I dreamt I saw your mother teaching a class
in which we all sat
    a little squeezed down in our seats.
She wore a hat
and under the brim her eyes burned
in and out,
her skull impossibly aflame
      under that power-mantle;
and our faces flushed
because we were ashamed,
who could not answer a single question
that she'd asked.

    And in the middle row
a woman had wet her pants, her head
hid in her arms;
      the urine flowing from her cunt
had puddled on the floor and seemed
the only sweetness in the room—
and we were drawn to her.

Although she was a spy,
she'd held the answers back,
    had changed her loyalty in our midst,
and in her effort wet herself
and I could taste
some curative
in her urine on the deck.

    The classroom was a ship—
Your mother
cracked her ruler on the wheel
her breath went in
and came out
acid accusation on the wind
and etched our faces
with these lines
of age and ignorance.

It was a sea dream—
and the ship meandered
and the uncontrolled woman took the helm
    and forced the cutter to its course
    and forced your mother
into staggering
underneath her crown, her power
now enfeebled,
    and our laughter,
now that we were cared for
ringing in her ears—
        who reeled against the railing
as the ship came in
and fled along the gangway
to the dock.

Her power-mantle lay
in the puddle of urine on the deck,
and as the ship took sail again
    our new teacher picked it up
and put it

like a tilted sailor's cap upon her head
and told us of another dream,
another sea tale
& awakening—

She
who from her endomorphic rage
woke up again, in the little lights
of altar candles
        and the cinnamon body oil,
and he who only dimly
thought that he had wakened her
                (could therefore
        place a cherry in her navel
and worry it with his tongue
in that slow way of his
while he was eating it)
could steer her into matrices
her husband had refused her;
        only the little body's exit
from her womb
as she had splayed herself
had given her
such power.

        And that he called her
"Goddess at whose feet I kneel"
annealed her
and she took him masterfully
into her own life, on her own terms.
And she was larger than he was
and huge to him,
        in translation of his mother's power
that lingered over him
                but in her flesh
became the mother he had always wanted.

        Wives are like our mothers / Fantan says /.
        When we were small our mothers fed us.

When we are grown our wives cook for us.
If there is something good,
they keep it in the pot until we come home.

When we were small we slept with our mothers;
when we are grown we sleep with our wives.
Sometimes
when we are grown
        we wake in the night
and call our wives
mother—

There you have
        pathology of the dream,
the teacher said, its politics—

But the woman lay
enchanted in her power, that place
where mothers die,
and the childish father that he was to her
        went up in incense smoke—
her tongue between his toes,
the forceful sucking of his sex.

And that he rightly felt
there is no root but this,
        no power and care.
He sucked her nipples for their juice;
they saw things in a clearer light
and eye to eye.

I woke
and thought of Kathy and the Old Manse,
        the way the woman had used
her diamond ring to carve
the message in the window glass:
futility of name and date,
her wedding night.
I'd made a joke

that didn't seem too funny when I woke,
that underneath the futile tracings
were the real words:
sex is life.

There was no other lesson
for me to take, except
I spend time at the sea
and if
within some sickness
        you became incontinent
I'd wipe your urine up
and I would suck the rag.

But the ship of love,
now powered by body's energy
        of such learning
in the coda of the dream
set out through fog (recessional)
to search
increasing clarity at sea.

And the Catholic, white
and summer knicker uniforms that we wore
        gave way to open classroom
as your mother's ruler
changed to a jeweled scepter on the desk
and was no longer a fearful weapon
but an instrument of charts—
        the newly hardening needle
of a human compass
that our new teacher
placed with reverence on the map.

The cutter banked
to a certain course against the sea,
        and as the ship came
momentarily broadside to the distant dock
we peered intently

from our childish comfort
at the windy rail,

and saw
the tortured, desperate woman
wave her hanky at us from the quay,
and we were waving also
as the ship turned
and she shrunk away,

and then we heard the ringing
of the school's little bells,
the peal, and falling of the leaves,

and we sang—

Goodby, Mother.
Goodby,

speck.

SEVEN POEMS

JOHN ALLMAN

ANNA O

> "From December 1880 to June 1882 Breuer treated what
> has become recognized as a classical case of hysteria, that
> of Frl. Anna O . . . her name . . . Bertha Pappenheim,
> deserves to be commemorated."—Ernest Jones, *The Life
> and Work of Sigmund Freud*

Can she open her throat? His hand smells of chloral,
      plunges in, like the girls
      who drown in Vienna's Canal.
On a muddy bottom where no one moves, he sticks a dead
needle in a dead arm. Is that the governess's poodle
      lapping water from his
      hand? She can't hold the orange.
It rolls toward him, off the bed, onto the floor, gleaming
in the sunlinght like his beard, like the goblets in the cabinet,
      a summer
      house
on fire. She squints everything into gray, taffeta
drapes, the rustle of his thighs. Outside on cobbles,
      the snap of whips,
      Papa sitting behind Talmud

and beard, heavy in his carriage, riding the Ringstrasse,
the circle of his wealth. Herr Doktor, no one ever dies.

And summer has its own musicians in a field, crackling
          a song, as the night train
          pierces the air. When was it
anyone with a family was happy? If she could walk, she'd
rub legs like a cricket, kick off blankets, run out
          in last year's brown dress
          turning green
with grass stains. Papa gasping on the pillow? Dead?
Really dead? She couldn't help him to the toilet, heal
          a lung,
          cough like a son.
If she could talk, she'd tell how Papa must run back,
flee the burning pit. She'd call the black dog
          wetting her leg
          Liebe. If she had
a life of her own, she'd walk through aunt's gold-frame
mirror, where the skull turns away, combing her hair.

She screams all morning. The healer doesn't come.
          He doesn't spoon
          his way through the words
that block her speech. Let his friend inject her
for the sake of sleep. Let him blow cigar smoke in her face,
          the mind's fog,
          while the blind
thing beats in her womb, kicks her side, claws to get out
and cries, falling backward in space. That's him
          running away. Do the men
          who touch her
always take feeling with them? The squint returns,
deafness like a door opening and closing, the arm limp
          as a snake. Something
          crowds her tongue.
Someone pulls down the skin beneath her eyes. She sees him
through a curtain of blood, the androgyne, without muscle.

Nothing sings like sleep. Nothing betrays like talk:
        white confessions
        carried in his black satchel,
dragged through Vienna's streets, public as Franz Josef's
court. She hears the coachman snoring in a cup, snuffling
        like a chaperone, asleep between
        daughter and father
who take in the Prater's green-tipped trees and sweet air.
The horses are smooth, draped with lilac. Last night,
        she freed a white bird
        trapped in a tree, she danced
alone, blooming in a swirl, running through the garden
between statues of men. When she woke, she was glad
        a white bird came near,
        that Papa doesn't suffer where he is.
In the world without men, her fear falls from everything,
fruit tumbles off the table, her fingers unfold to the sun.

TALKING TO THE APES

The universal sign for what is unknown
        is a kind of shrug, lowered
brow; a shaking of the wrist so that
        fingers clash. Nodding
the head may or may not signify
        approval. Ticks, fleas,
the usual intimates of arboreal life
        die the same death beneath
any nails. The thick-skinned orange
        gives a roundness to the air

not available in mountains, but common
        to the shape of endearment.
Hugging, scratching, grooming is allowed
        in fullness behind bushy

silence. A tree stripped to bone is
    whiteness. Who doesn't require
the sound of water? A brimming cup tilts
    always. Now one must agree on
"pour." This is the meaning of rain. Sky
    descends. Rivers will not stay.

The region of thighs is known by the sign
    for "itch," but different from
what is considered by certain thinkers as
    intrinsic. Which of us would be
evolving? The baring of the teeth brings forth
    an orange, or hanging
upside-down. In the sunlight, notice
    how he disavows the gesture
for "serve." And how someone must either
    clean or abandon the latrine.

FISH

Their transparent bones like ridges
    along a young girl's spine;
a flexing in currents turning warm
    in casual affinity
with spillways of blood. Is it blood
    pricked from the finger by a
gill, ecstasy that writhes in milky
    threads? If one of us
had to be downright, lipping bladder-
    wrack, the other had to drown.

And we hear of the boy washed ashore,
    his blue tongue the color
of stripes along highbrow angelfish
    who seem to gulp for air.

Nothing is truly lost: a tentative
      gain in weeds that
snake toward the sun through green
      lake water. Or milky pods
of last year's poppies broken into
      by awkward thumbs.

Why should we sing so loud about walking
      upright? Or is it opposable
thumb, tool, repeatable sound for "mud"
      and "rock" that divides footprints
from the vacancies in water left by hurrying
      sturgeon? Look at the children
walking three abreast, questioning the sun,
      letting their voices glide
where the tide slips back toward deep-fisted
      creatures. Hands rising to light.

THE EXCURSION

Arriving, we are told the fare is free
& we step backwards out of the bus.
The sign says, "Do Not Look Behind You."
We hold up our pocket mirrors and smile,
watching our shabby grandfathers wave
as an Immigration Officer misspells
their names for life. Boys in dark caps
are eating dark bread. We bite our lips,
wince at odors of cheese and urinals,
& hear of the wives left behind,
drowned in wells. A man points to the harbor
but we cannot hear what he says. Go back?
The sign blinks on: "Give Your Mirrors A Rest."

Time for lunch, back to back, talk forbidden.
We sip orange drinks. The dry sandwiches

stick to our teeth already turning black.
One of us faints. Porters carry him away.
We are not permitted to turn around,
the notes go from hand to hand,
don't, don't, don't. The PA tells us to stand,
do deep-knee bends, run in place.
Faster. Faster. Loose change falls to the floor.
Children begin to cry. Our double time
shakes the sign off the wall.
One of us falls to his knees, weeping.
We comfort him. We sing the national anthem.

Our bus driver grins, greeting us outside,
the sign on his chest: "Exact Fare Required."
He says we'll get a free box dinner. We grin.
We exchange our mirrors for souvenir buttons.
A woman in a tweed suit has a ten-dollar bill
& two men walking backwards take her away.
A child cries for his mother & we give him
an aunt, a bag of peaches, a toy whistle,
& the PA says whoever's lost will be found.
Someone says, "Isn't this nice?" "What time is it?"
We're all seated now. The doors slap closed.
The bus pulls out onto a dark road, trees brush
our windows like drowning hands, we close our eyes.

THE REAL INSPECTOR

The real inspector poked me
in the ribs. "No wound," he said.
I lifted the bullet to his nose.
"Only hearsay evidence, sir."
This was a kind of defeat.
I sat down. I was innocent.
The inspector scratched his head.
"Once more, sir, if you don't mind."

He punched me in the side. I gasped.
He found it: a small-caliber
tunnel to my lungs. "Very clean, sir,
a regular work of art." Could I breathe?
The inspector lit a match.
Looked in. A voice sang out.
His whiskers turned to ice.
"Something's there," he said.

I saw the bulge beneath his mackintosh.
"You don't really carry a . . . ?"
He chewed his mustache. "Sorry,
sir, it's just my job.
Shall we try it again?"
He plunged his hand into my side,
the wind rushed through his fingers,
my nerves hummed like harps.
A small bird hopped on a rib.
It peeped. The inspector
backed away and smiled.
"You understand," he said,
"it's still hearsay."
He tipped his bowler, ta ta,
climbed out the window,
and I began to sing.

A POEM GREW ROUND

A poem grew round, fat, obsequious.
I ran inside it. I checked the dials
in the curved walls: altimeter at 000;
fuel down to ½; water pouring up out of a glass.
No G. I wasn't going anywhere in this heat.
So I rolled out of the poem
& slipped down the cellar stairs.
There they were, rows of pumpkins

collapsing like faces in the subway.
I said, this is too easy, & poked
my hand through a soft orange cheek,
I heard a voice, *my god I can't stand it!*
while roots grew hairy in the dark.
I growled & raced out the back door,
sniffing rocks, the mock orange,
I snapped the dogwood until it bled
such odors! This is illegal!
I saw the clematis crawling up my house.
No wonder I couldn't breathe.
How could I get the poem out the door?
I'd never measured it & now it was
fetid, half-gassed, bloated, useless
as the furnace of a dead sun or
a pumpkin in orbit, worse than a dream
of cucumbers in the gutters of Fifth Street.

ASTRONAUTS AND THE DANCER

Descended from a no-G chamber
on the lip of a dusty crater
they struggle through windless nights
in clumsy air-tight suits and weighted shoes
taking photos of a shadow you never
leave behind   they cannot explain the torn
space they follow you through where the left
becomes the right   matter is reversed
they see your head turn like an owl completely
around   your mouth speaking from your forehead
their cameras take the same pictures of themselves
upturned children walking on their hands
while you enter rocks and disappear emerging behind
them   they turn slowly to face backwards always
facing each other hopelessly   even as they reach
forward their hands move in wrong directions

they keep walking downhill on their hands
the pain presses upon them where they cannot
locate the nerves not responding as you dance
into a warp of mirrors leading to the sun
your silhouette a shadow your blackness is
expanding to all of space enclosing them
closing like the iris-rent they came through
now lost forever reversed finding there is
nowhere to go

TEN DRAWINGS

MIHAIL CHEMIAKIN

Introduced by Aleksis Rannit

Is Mihail Chemiakin a New Prince of Paris?

Aleksis Rannit

For Thomas P. Whitney

It was around 1950 that the American reaction against Paris and French art took place in an aesthetically convincing manner. France had gracefully but firmly dominated fine arts for over two hundred years, but it was clear that she was already organically exhausted. True, some significant French artists, like Braque and Matisse, were still alive, but stylistically they already belonged to the living past. —Is not art of vital importance brought about only as a concurrence of passion, talent, and erudition? —The French probably will never lose their erudition, but the new noted painters who appeared after the Second World War—Mathieu, Bazaine, Estève, Manessier, and Soulages—could produce merely textural sophistication or tectonic decorativeness and not living art. They could hardly rival the Americans Mark Tobey, de Kooning, Kline, Rothko, and Motherwell, who actually created a new expressive artistic sensibility and thus modified our ways of seeing. There was one single exception, however: Nicholas De Staël, at once an abstractionist and a realist, who was born into an aristocratic Baltic

19

family in St. Petersburg, educated in Brussels, and later moved to France, became the last deep radiance of the French sunset in plastic arts. De Staël's painting was a humanist and artistic miracle, a miracle interrupted by his suicide at the age of forty-three. Not only did he know how to reduce a multitude of large forms to resonant architectural units of electrifying colors, he added to Parisian modernist painting a dynamically serene tonality and created a metaphysical space not present in French art since the death of Odilon Redon in 1916. After the departure of De Staël in 1955, a darkness of trivia descended on both French painting and the painting of the École de Paris, that non-French school originally created by the legendary foreigners Picasso, Gris, Modigliani, De Chirico, Pascin, Brancusi, Van Dongen, Soutine, Foujita, Giacometti, Dali, Miró, Wiiralt, Chagall, and others who ignited the flame of experimentalism in France.

It took about two decades for the sad landscape of Parisian art to brighten again. This happened with the arrival in the French capital in 1971 of a Russian underground painter, Mihail Chemiakin (who pronounces his name *Shemiakin,* and occasionally signs himself Michel de Chemiakine). Chemiakin, who had worked as a simple loader and handyman in Leningrad's Hermitage Museum, had, in 1964, secretly arranged an exhibition of his own there, taking down paintings of a certain collection and replacing them with his own works. During the three days of bureaucratic confusion this caused, Chemiakin's paintings were on view. Then the exhibition was closed, the artist thrown out, and the administratively responsible curator dismissed. Be that as it may, Chemiakin became a famous case in the international press. His next big publicity came from Madame Dina Vernay, the last model and confidante of Aristide Maillol. She was able to take a collection of Chemiakin's engravings and drawings out of the Soviet Union in 1971, and arranged his first one-man exhibition abroad in her own renowned art gallery in Paris. Alain Bosquet and other French men of letters rushed to celebrate him, and Chemiakin was soon well established in France. Later he received recognition in Germany, Switzerland, Japan, and South America, although his reputation in the United States has been restricted to a fairly small circle.

Chemiakin's medium-size paintings first give the impression of lost mythical frescoes of the pre-classical world. One immediately recognizes the allegorical, symbolic, and ritualistic character of these compositions. They are painted in broken colors and look like

old tapestries. Notwithstanding their subtle *coloris,* particularly in
the early silver-toned examples, the presence of linearity is strongly
evident. Especially convincing and most congenial to Chemiakin's
talent is the style of his India-ink drawings, like those made in the
Greek island town of Hydra in 1977–78, ten of which—hitherto
unpublished and never exhibited—are reproduced here. What
strikes one immediately about them is an elegance of conception
expressed by manneristic yet, strangely enough, simple execution.
There is nothing superfluous, nothing common, nothing trivial, al-
though there is a certain concentration on the fanciful and gro-
tesque. From the smallest drawing to the largest—a sheet of paper
filled with some twenty designs composed as a flux or, rather, a
diary of visions—these works seem complete in every detail, inevi-
table, without limitation of time, or labor, or thought. It is possible
that the drawings, streaming as if from a horn of plenty, express an
aspect of the idea that an image shares the essence of its living
original, namely, that by multiplying the images, one causes the
living things themselves to multiply. Notwithstanding such strong
surges of ideas and images, the line is well-ordered, pure, and
clean, as in Botticelli's drawings for the *Divine Comedy,* or perhaps
even purer in the technical sense, since Chemiakin, unlike Botticelli
or Beardsley, for example, only occasionally applies any pressure
of pen. The pen, held lightly, glides over the surface of the paper
with the eurythmic felicity of a classical dancer.

Whatever their precise allegorical meaning, Chemiakin's figures
of antiquity, often resembling the low reliefs called "coelanglyphic,"
seem to this writer to be not carefree Olympians but the symbolic
embodiment of some metaphysical truth. Sensual as they are, they
have, beyond all the delicacy of variety, an air of power and com-
mand, and yet they remain an expression of sympathetic magic.
Chemiakin tries to reconcile the great known and unknown forces
governing the ancient and modern world. He, the artist-sorcerer,
enacts rites in the mysterious movements of his flowing lines. In
his works the graphic and fantastic aspects are dominated by the
harmony of the whole decorative and structural effect and of the
coherence of the elements of his esoterics and aesthetics. And why
should we wish to disassociate thaumaturgical utility from artistic
spontaneity? There is no more incompatibility between them than
between religious faith and creative intuition. Chemiakin's realistic
representation (he is an enemy of abstract art) is based on a prin-
ciple that is often applied unconsciously. His concern is not with

what he sees in a subject, but what he knows is there; his realism is therefore intellectual. —Did Lascaux, Altamira, Mesopotamia, Egypt, and Greece (of the earliest archaic period as well as the latest Hellenistic style) contribute to his metapsychological and stylistic ideas?

Chemiakin appeared in Paris at the right time. He is the most French of the Russian artists, even more so than Russian-born Frenchmen like Benois and Lanceray, who contributed a great deal to the St. Petersburg culture of the twentieth century. Russian by his nationality, French by his place in art (is not Mary Cassatt American—her art French?), Mihail Chemiakin is today the new prince of Paris. Like his predecessor, Jean Cocteau, who was also—for half a century—called the prince of Paris and who liked besides to term himself "le prince frivole," the easy and versatile Chemiakin is learned but carries his learning lightly. Like Cocteau, he is an elegant exhibitionist; like Cocteau, he possesses a kind of Raphaelic immateriality of style; and, like Cocteau, he is brilliant and lucid, but at the same time mystifies and, of course, hides himself behind the mask of a *saltimbanque*. His message, too, is a message to cultured society, and his mission, however hieratic he may become, is not unlike Cocteau's—to give pleasure and to surprise. The polished jewelry of Gallic reflection is present in his finest drawings, as is the certainty of intellectual delight, the French grace of workmanship. The problem of nationality in art is, nonetheless, a complicated one, and Chemiakin himself, being a cultural Russian nationalist (without any trace of Russian emotionalism in his style), may well challenge my attribution. For as the poet Marina Tsvetaeva wrote on July 6, 1926, to Rainer Maria Rilke, who had dedicated an elegy to her: "To create a poem means to translate from the mother tongue into another language . . . No language is the mother tongue. For that reason I do not understand when people speak of French or Russian poets. A poet can write in French, but he cannot be a French poet . . . Orpheus exploded and broke up the nationalities, or stretched their boundaries so wide that they now include all the nations, the dead and the living."

The ten India-ink drawings that follow are all taken from the Hydra Island Cycle, 1978–79, in the artist's own collection.

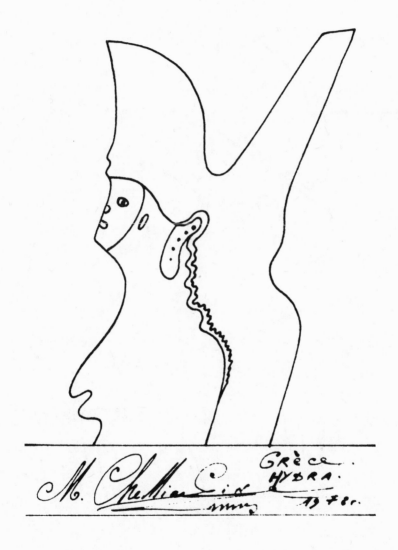

GRÈCE.
HYDRA.

1980.

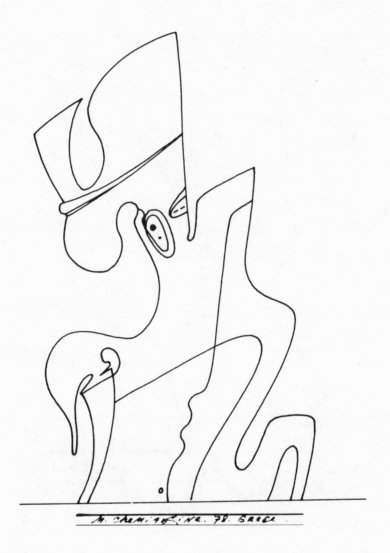

M. Chemiakine. 78. Grece.

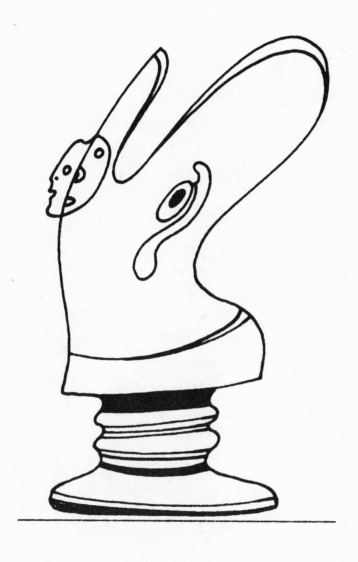

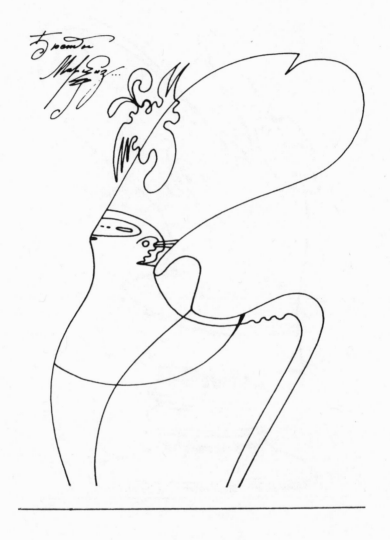

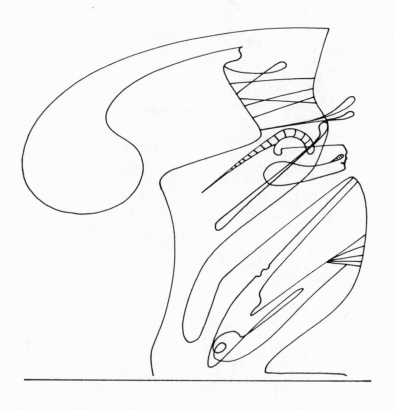

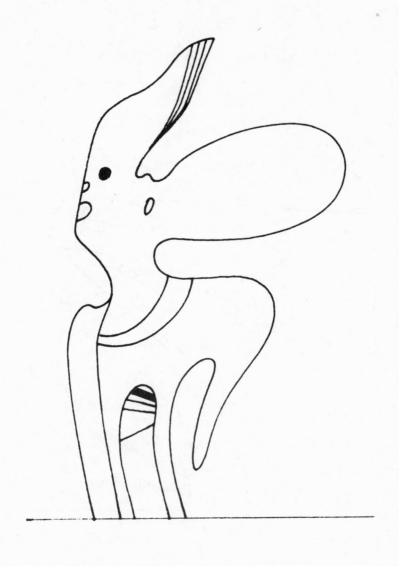

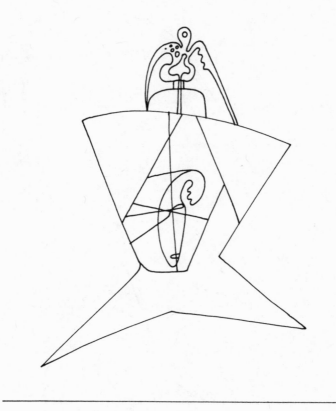

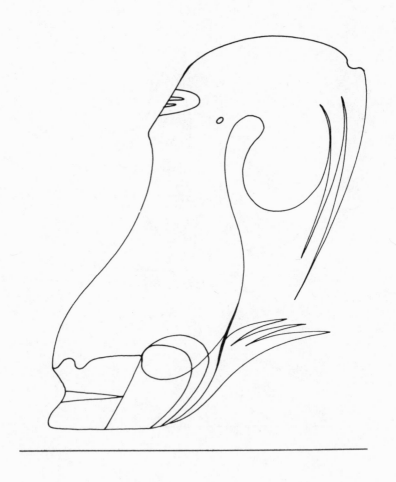

AN ALTERNATE LIFE

ROBERT DUNCAN

IN THE SOUTH

Tears will not start here.   The mountain I see
—misty, ascending—weighs in as if it were a cloud,   is not here;
it is louder, though soundless, than the magpie's song.

Dawn did not start here.   The heart I stand
whose need of you   will obey *your* sense of the right and wrong of it
—for, ultimately, there must be in our geometries—
needs many lives   —a meeting place thruout.

Am I so darkend   no ray of the sun will venture?
No will   rays out to touch the release waiting?
No hand reaches or would reach to verify,
quickening into its actual earth element   the visual mountain?

        •

I am talking about the beginnings of an age in my body,
light as a mountain   hanging in the air
no one may lift   from me.   In youth
I think now   this fathering shadow   fell forward
from every glance   drawing to ward me   alarms,
        turnings,   alternate engagements,   what compells.

33

It is a heavy light shining I am speaking of.
Visibly I am moving over to the other side of the picture.
An old man's hand fumbles at the young man's crotch.
An old man's body is about to tremble.   The painter
is almost cruel in his detail to make clear
this shaking.   I am talking of a voice shaking.

I am shaking the rattling gourd of infancy's play.
At the sombre coda of the natural symphony,
what sweet sweeping memorials the violins impart,
more vigorous than ever   the brassy crescendos,
the drumbeat of the heart penetrates all.   O, yes,
Love will at last let go of me.   Let go of me!
I don't want any longer to wait for the thematic release.

Still. .   as if all the sound were gone into me. .
this sound alone,   the rattling gourd of first things,
so faintly sounds,   plaintive and falling away.

    •

        Morning flows over me.   The cold
        washes up against the warmth of me.
        I stretch my limbs into it.

        The new age almost fades from my limbs.
        All my old youth stretches out to fill my flesh.

        Up.   Up.   The skin is singing!
        This skin   addresses the day where I am.

    •

Tho you were only an incident in an alternate life,
and there I was,   as the Lover always is,
swift, leading,   seeking to release the catches of your shirt,
broody, sweet,   tendering the flame of hurt in the healing,

here, in the one life I am leading, I am,

as the Lover always is,   alone before a hand that holds forth
the burning of a heart for me to eat again.

                        For the sake of the Beloved
in this world   the Everlasting instructs.   I crouch
to eat out the bitter heart from that withholding hand again.

·

The Mind   —the fucking Mind!   The stars in Its thought
shine forth in abysses, "Night"spaces,
the fucking alone brought us *deep* into.

·

Circling,   circling,   circling, the matter of Love
the Mind knows   has my own particular death in it.
Wary the predator I am   watches to surprise
the moment when   this hunger will yield in me.

Lovely, ever,   this hunting eye's look of you.
In the alternate life I am visiting early Spring again.
Nothing is revised.   I am again without help.

This matter of Love the Mind knows   has
inconsequential ecstasies in its teasing of Time.

Circling,   circling, I can no longer spell the word
the beast I follow might have said to me.

It is not "Death",   not my own particular time of dying.
So many alternate lives have died in me.
I wake this morning searching for the Life I knew,
like a cemetery in the sun searching,
surrounded by yew trees,   bathed in the blaze of light
and the wash of the sky's blue.

But that is the little graveyard in Soquel
where you and I walkt together years ago,
and that blue of sky is not today's alternative
but what *really* was,   "ours",   I had forgotten.

Here where the tears long stored up will not really start,
it is really raining.   It is almost cold.

The cars rushing past the open door
hiss in the gleam of the road beyond.
There is no full blaze of light.   It comes thru the downpour.

.

And "I" come forward to gaze into the downpouring glass,
the black crystal in which I find the world
looking for "me".   I hide in my looking.

When we sit down to dinner, I will put the looking-glass away.
I will put away watching for the furtive movement in the flesh
that betrays what I know is hidden there.
    I will give up   this stalking time,
and we will converse of arts and informative reveries.

.

So I love what is "real".   How awkwardly we name it:
the "actual", the "real", the "authentic"—What Is.

I have come to it as if I could have been "away",
flooded thru by the sorrow of the unlived, the unanswerd,
tho I knew not and had not the courage of asking
    the question that calld for it,
the real I *did* see.   The real so toucht me

    I could not speak before it.

HOMECOMING

Now truly the sexual Eros will have
    left me and gone on his way.
It is a superstition of our time that
    this sexuality is all,   is
lock and key,   the body's
    deepest sleep and waking.

At break of day and at
    midnight's time of play
you are turnd away from me.

       And for Love's sake
I once in mounting raptures of my flesh, in
    singing nerves and mouthing quest,
gatherd up
    the ache and spring of Life
into Love   however I could
    make it with you,
I now lie in a dark of my own,
    nursing my body's unquiet watch.

Angel of this tristesse,
what would you prepare me for?
Nothing is broken.   He. .   you. .
will still hold my hand and
    sound me where I am.
The dearness alone lights my eyes I feel.

Not until the meaning of our
    house so changes me
would I read thru to what you mean.

Is it Time?   How I attend
the *"now"* of it,   then in every attention
momentous.   It is the impending
I address as messenger.   Under the
sullen weight of an increase in Time

the hour carries, all,   but my body
heavier than the time it occupies,
        would surrender.

                •

It would be a marvel I might await
if I were here—in my eighth set of seven years
        completed, my ninth beginning—
brought into a new teaching.

But this news I brought forward with me thru Time
        reaching so into what is ours
I knew in the beginning in myself.   You
did not institute its orders I have come to know.

Lockt in its solitary vise, its appetite,
the carnal body of me climbd upon your spirit
to light   the darkness wanted out of you.   For company?
A flame?   An ember still?   Bright   solitary eyes,
unseeing,   seek their terminals in Night.

And it seems I cradled in this stare.
It was my share you first accepted to be ours
of me, this unwonted need I have so worn
I know no longer if it be truly there.

                •

This is my first and final place,
    in the outlands of the sun's decline,
            this dark of the sexual moon,
this cold and shadow
        home   in Time.

            And I, ardent and would-be
                artful talker,   of
            winged words,   birds or arrows
                sing thru the air,   soar up
                    not for song alone

this war and this return

but for their end in Time.

·

"*La politique des vieux,*"
it came to me to say in this
    first session of talking in French:
"*C'est leur vengeance contre la vie.*"

—la vengeance de la Vie   contre ma vie—

"*Et moi,   je suis maintenant
        dans le foyer de cet âge.*"

For Time has come into a new age.

    La veille de ma vieillesse
—fitting that this announcement should come
        in language I do not know to speak,
the marches of the day
        inexpert thruout.   The risk of the wrong
words must charge thru.
                                Another
        has always been here,
            keeping this watch,
dry-eyed,   to scrutinize
        what I dare not see as I go,   weigh
            even the thought-to-be-inconsequential
in the outcome,   exact of it
        the very ache and spring from which
            it thought to come

    to this place,   this *home*-ground,

        this place alone. .

                I was always there
. . .*not there.*

SUPPLICATION

> Let me have the grace to speak of this
> for I would mind what happens here.

Tears came   no more than the token   eyes
  gathering in   to mind the heart
  swells to the brim   yet I savor the loss.

So swift the alternate continent drifts from under.
  Unalterably this plane   carries me in its course.

There was no might-have-been,   there is
  only the one thing   this   I go   to ward

keep of my soul-enforcing   —remembering the kiss.

  Do I really want the thunder of this hour,
this mouth my mouth seeks,   this tongue
  my tongue addresses,   this Word

to come so entirely into the core of Being?

He, not I,   *he* was shaking.   He did not mean
  to corner this feeling.   We will never
      advance   to ward each other.

Who am I?   so alien
  to the courses of his youth?   in the wrong?

  •

The moment is spectral and I gather it to be
a part I must play in this stage   not my own
yet forever now in this playing   a part of me
drawn into the pattern of a lordly pretension
the coming forth of the body by day is.

So swift the time-flow drifts away from under,

yet how the filament of continued feeling goes out
to touch upon what's lost from view.

How can I see so   the curve of your lips,
the lilt hear of your sounding of English,
    so far from mine,
and catch again in the glance of eyes   a thrill of being
upon the edge of that panic   I wonder. .
something here divines me,   finds me out.

The very doubt of living upon which Life
from its initial darings casts itself abroad
I hear rehearse again   its monologue
meant for the communion of all souls   in you.

            •

        Another plane.   Another time returning home.

Another over-view.   What in me

        reaches toward you again and yet, in reaching,

recognizes itself in these ranges,

        these majesties,   these desolations,

            this wilderness,   far below?

        •

Far as the eyes can reach,   the land
        reaches beyond.   The mind
            sees arms of land reaching out to sea.

Far as the sea's reaches, in the dissolve of horizons,
        the mirage of voyage extends
—the imagined discoveries,   the foreign shores,
        the ports of call,   the shipwrecks, unreal islands,

the being cast adrift,   the drownings—
as if we recalld the nature of the deep
out of what we were.   O terra firma,   terra infirma,

receive me as you will.   Let me
return,   entirely yours,
even to the ununderstandable,
the mountainous urgencies,   the eroding tides,
this continent,   this age,

let me. .
return me. .

We near the gate and the towers of the city.

This mirage of thronging powers and lives,
of thoroughfares and those bridges
glittering in the sun,   everywhere
addresst to the presiding prospect of this bay,
wherein the resolution of our watch and ward
be realized,
let me return.

O   daily actual life   entirely what I've known,

companion and familiar to my love,

admit what I am   deep in your thrall.

THE QUOTIDIAN

There is no way that daily I have not been
initiate.
The admission is all.

At last it comes,   rising from the other side
in me,   the unalterd

resolution,   my affair with the beginnings of this world
      held to the last
governor of an ever-returning coda,   the daily rituals:

the unfolding, the stretching, the turning upon the spine,
   surfacing,   breathing in the day's air,
   conscious,   opening eyes to steal
a look entirely mine of you
  —delicious, how
        ever close it is to first seeing,
the feeling of this awakening,

this stealing of a life-fire,   of this
   Promethean infancy,
from the foundaries of a parental embrace,
   up from the debris of dreams
        into the body desire prepared
to rise again from its own ashes—

   familiar,   strange,   familiar,

just here,   this joyous quietude,

already troubled by the falling away
   of remnants of another life
      into Lethe.

     •

I do not speak here of that river
   you read to be an allusion
      to ancient myth and poetry,
though it too belongs to a story,
but of a rushing underground of the very life-flow,
   a sinking-back,
      a loss of the essential in the
shadows and undertow—

from which I come up into the day time.

The bedside radio I turnd on just as I woke
announces the minute of the hour.

     In the realm of this mind I return to
the steps of the sun have already
   set into motion and number
     the rememberd measures.

Seven o'clock in the morning renews itself over breakfast
  —the richness of coffee, the full flavor of the bread
     toasted, the assorted jams and marmalades—   we
initiate the naming of the day
  with the institution of a choice of things
    and repetitions of our way,   yet
altering minutely the course of decisions   thruout

     design   and unalterable variations.

   •

I speak here of riding the earth
round into the sunlight again,

of this "It came to pass that. . ."
in which we take place   ours, swift,

inevitable, answering   this   current
turning upon the axis of another year,

this ever
growing older in turning

    into Spring again,
coming into Easter,   into the
  passions of resurrection,   the commingling
     of life-streams in this
ceremony of pouring,
  into the precession of equinoxes in the Great Year
     to the flowering insurrections of Aquarius.

•

One more week and it will be here
    still   "It",   the persistence I seem to
draw this "I" from.   The one
    fountain, Memory   —the other,
        Lethe, the Healer. .   The two waters
pour forth from the mouth of It.
                        The wars,
    the rage for the retribution of wrongs,
        the Easter Man upon his cross,
the successions of loss and love
    found anew,   the stroke,
        the demolition of all goods,
the contest with evil,   the communal joy—
        pass on.

            They were what we volunteerd,
        incidents the mind barely recalls.

                        Let me then
        recite the seasons as I would recite
            the passing of anarchists and great kings.

        Lovely now
                news comes from the South,
        gifts from another time I
            most hold in losing.   Did I really
        take place there?
                    In that history too?

        Down under the seasons I know?

        •

        It goes as it will.
        Its haunt is an edifice of air
        most sound in what we do not hear   but draw
        from out of whose invisibilities
        illustrious hints of visage where

our human faces come to light,   a music
our music might steal away from.   I'd make
my way   in strains of song   to you
as ever.   Let the aweful rivers
come through into the one bed,
the momentary coursing.

Take your time with me.
I belong to it.

Daily the minutes pass.   The hours
return into themselves.   The first time seems
already worn.   The wear
yields to transformations of the air,
I long for its verging upon meaning so.

Unbearable,   the pathos into
    beauty of this theme,

the changes,   the constancy.

                ●

Every day I am away,   I remember.
The night of each day lapses into a deepening of gold.
Everyday gods of the ordinary preside even in dreams and hold
the keys of the locks from which this language flows.

Every day these household conduits and currents, these
    circulations of water and of fire.
Every day the shadow of this mountain grows in the mind.
Every day, in the alembic of an increasing time come due,
    glows and quickens into an instant flare to ash
    this mountainous desire
and prolongs youth's passionate realities—bright spectral residue—
into this dim reminder in which Life aches to die
    and, lasting, watches every day pass by.

In youth   what did I know?
The violence of a fierce weather shook me so
I could not move for it   or rusht abroad
as if my soul were all fire and rain mixt in a cloud.

Love I would not have allowd
alone could release the soul of what I was to be
I sought in the flaming up of sexuality
yet, raging in the beauty of the flower,
tore at the heart before the fruit to be devourd devourd
    what was.

Here, in the foyer of my age,
the passing of the storm remains upon the page
where I reread myself   and all
that once befell comes once again to fall.
It is a text of after-images.

There was a rumor of me I almost overheard
I now construct from word to word
a song that in the alternate life I pourd
forth upon the radiant air that my world with me be stirrd.

Man's a bird of omen, dark as anthracite, upon that golden bough,
and all his words, the rapturous reiteration of some vow,
an animal call in anguish, a summoning of fate,
in which the strife,   the wearing   and the after-glow
of what was realized,   the total thrust of a life,

charges the contour of a momentary line
as if throughout we meant but to sign   this place and time.

　　　　　•

Every day that I am here   I recall
early notes in the sounding of the late.

What we have shared, our life in me,
the leavings and returnings of these years,

withdrawn from what bright multiplicities
prepared.
                Love
that overtakes me and pervades the falling of the light

    touches upon a presence that is all.

TWO POEMS

JEROME ROTHENBERG

VIENNA BLOOD

For Herman Hakel

1

like carneval
for street & house
our action holds the place
between   the women
guard the door
no longer
they rush into the squares
& find
Vienna in the night
a jewless
hauptstadt city without
rime or grace
the others have survived in
alone   who stand
—friend Hakel—
muted cattle dumb
& lost

the darkness is their own
now   there is no one
can do again the thing
we did   the victim
dies
the mothers cannot
heal this birth
disorder of the town
where Hitler walked
he saw (sweet shadow) looming
the devil   Jew
my grandfather
this one could be
who scared him
shitless to Linz he ran
there buried
his face in the whipped cream
linzer torts
his momma saved for him
& roared
—o triumph of the will—
—disasters of the modern state—
the gentile's mind
is dumb & cruel
the song says
proven right

2   *The Danube Waltz*

I found a river
in Chicago
here I found one not
until the last day
on road to "airport"
saw it unwinding
saw it alongside
the left side
of the bus   how pale

& shy
thy houses
far from the architecture
built by empire
to its gods kings ministers of finance
waltzing
waltzing
in your grave
where is thy river
& thy woods
so old   like Jews
forever gone
we walk too among ghosts
the sounds of poetry
(ka ka)
the only music left us
arises still in Jandl's voice
a Jewish loaf still sold
at Neumarkt drowned out
still by waltzes
hokey
pokey
in shadow of thine arches
emperors have sat
the little cousins sit now
holding hands
the river (distant) waltzes on
to Budapest   between
thy left & right

3

the carnevals of middle
Europe blaze
the fetes bring
destroyers of a million worlds
to dance
by torchlight to punk rock

how heavy at night
their bodies are
& shine
their innocence is brutal
boots & belts
even the young ones wear
the artists
who carve crosses in their flesh
they lead us drunk
into Croatian bars
the German boy
sings Yiddish:
Rayzeleh
mine sheyneh
so jealous of
the sufferings of others
must inflict their own

4

the liminal   he writes
or "place between"
& sees   suddenly
the terror of that situation
terror in glass
in camphor
the eye inside his eye
looks back
finding the place he shades off
is not himself
now is not
some other self
insistent
feels like shit
& wonders:
at edge of what dark city
will he stop?
what phantom turning

that dark edge
also will stop
& stop him?
or Blake
"the draught of violence
"that draws extinction in"
uncertainty: a zone
a fruitful chaos
& the sacred's what's inside
the frame
(but what's inside it
if the terror
isn't there?
or what's inside *me*
if I play the prince
in Nerval's tower
reading my poems in heart of
empty Europe
—luckless—
knowing too well these things
but hoping   like Artaud
"to break through language
"in order to touch life")
INSTRUCTIONS:
make a circle
around a tree
ring bells
cut sacred time out
live in it
a moment
doing everything
all senses
into play
be flexible
& playful
nothing fixed
but improvised
to name: all time   all space
reversing roles

where all is open
—flowing—
the light shades off
the darkness
not yet complete

5

For Victor Turner

communitas
(I meant to tell you)
is holy terror

THE SECRET DREAM OF JACOB FRANK

> "So in Poland for the first time I did things which no one
> knows   for these were things which the lips cannot
> utter   The heart keeps them to itself"
> —J.F., *The Sayings of the Lord*

remembered
he is your counterpart   the other
Jew transgressor
of their law
moves to the performance of
your dream
the synagogues he stalks thru
wrecked & helpless
scrolls thrown down
this madman   nihilist
once mounted
pissed 'gainst the parchment
howling
he would lisp in mockey yiddish

banged shutters
where our wise men—sages—slept
"I am the crow"
(he cried)
"the cock in frenzy
"will fly past Reno
"to my wedding
"secrets of the faith lead me
"to the Queen of Germany
"her Jews will plot against me
"screams will follow
"when I leave her
"far off in time
"remembered in prison
"I am a simple man
"delaying
"stood me on the table
"saw the abyss below
"fell thru to it
but wakened
further off the lady
lingered
mad astrologer
her body danced to his
all night
kept waking
making entrances
"again I meet you mistress
"in Bohemia
"the clocks are cookoo here
"the floors of bedrooms
"shine with hearts
"the ceilings
"painted with red hearts
"& heart-shaped mirrors
"near your bed
"so slavic like the maids
"who feed us
"I messiah Jacob Frank

"am in the center of
"a giant heart
"my member raised to strike
"thee my shekinah bride
"on eiderdowns
"thou leans to me
"thy mouth is like a birdcage
"—lock me up in it!—
"& swallow floods of love
"like chicken drippings
"passed from mouth to mouth
"the tongue of me messiah Jacob Frank
"is on the tongue of thee
"Shekinah Lilith Lady of the North
he said   like simple man
had brought two ladders to her roof
& climbed them
Queen Shekinah looks down
from her painted cloud
her heavens filled with horses
he can mount
the door into her bosom
opens   closes
riding the sky the sun
is now a man
he stares at you then turns
back to the lady
they will fly off together
waving *la*
dee da they sing
the advent of Italian opera
stirs the cantors
dirty songs become
G-d's words
my little honey girl
—he sings &
hugs the torah—
I am raw with love
& catch you

by the river I will snatch
your books
will walk beside the shores
150 wagons
wait on
for the simple man
robe bundled on his head
who swims across
jeering faces of Rumanians
abuse him
their corn mush weighs him down
"sweet Jews
(he says)
"my journey is my own
"my dreams are thine
"o little g-d
"the image of my lady floats still
"over head
"she sister to the sun
"will lend a horse to me
"crosswise from channel
"I have sprung
"to land in Bukavina
"home of thieves
"in spades
"in diamonds
raises his fists
with cards hard at the flush
cut gems whose value
no one knows
our leader!
say the thieves
our little g-d!
& welcome him
around their fires drinking
their sour wines
now tells his visions:
armies of Jewish gonnifs
march with him

on roads to Warsaw
the women sing
a queen steps forward
she leaves the gentile crowd
to give him
hand of his daughter once again
wise one she calls him
master jew
he beats his drum hard
daughter & shekinah become one
beside him in his wagon
—hauled by demented bears—
but the lovers
speak in Polish   Turkish
is their second tongue
the gentiles stand in awe
sounds of entwining serpents
in their ears
their wallets lined with stone
caverns of metropolis appear
trains like comets
down its streets
the wagon moves beneath the "el"
to make a living
they will sell new knives
to wives & daughters
"o the lives of Jews are hard
(the song goes)
"even the messiah sits
"in shit
"beside the sewers   screws
"an eye toward heaven
lady fades
the sun in darkness shuts
his only lid
box buried in the earth
her catholic angels sing
"hosanna"
in the speech of mice

THE NIGHT OF THE GRYLA

WILLIAM HEINESEN

Translated from the Danish by Hedin Brønner

TRANSLATOR'S NOTE. *The Faroese poet-novelist William Heinesen was presented to the American public in ND38, which contained his bacchanalian story "The Flies: Symphonic Variations for Strings and Wind, Percussion and Insecticides"—a surrealistic cry against war and militarism. His tale about the mystic ritual of the Gryla (pronounced "Gree'-la") and her amazing phallus is quite as mad in concept, but in style so different that it could well be taken for the work of another author. It is one of the many marks of Heinesen's genius that he so easily swings between the wildest excesses and the starkest simplicity of language.*

"The Night of the Gryla" is loosely based on ancient Norse folklore which survived in the Faroe Isles until recent times. But apart from the central idea of a Gryla ("howler" or "growler") it is all Heinesen—the pathos and sly humor, the characters and setting, the implied social comment, the curious human twist—all heinesenesque in its very essence. Needless to say, Stapa is a fictitious place name. The time of the action is the early part of this century.

William Heinesen was born in 1900 and is still going strong, working on yet another addition to his great store of intellectual fireworks—this time a volume of stories. The complex circumstances that move him to write in Danish rather than his cherished native Faroese were explained in the note preceding "The Flies."

The present story, titled "Grylen" in the original, is from William Heinesen's collection Det fortryllede lys *("The Enchanted Light"), published by Gyldendal, Copenhagen, in 1957. It appears now for the first time in English.—H.B.*

This is the story of the Gryla on the isle of Stapa, a strange creature that will not be easy to describe. Not by any means. For no one knows the Gryla except Young Dunald, and his lips are sealed with seven seals. Even if he wanted to tell about it he would not be able to, for he is no man of words. His spirit has other ways of unfolding. His joy is that of the dancing calf, his sadness that of the molting bird. His belief in himself is matched only by that of the Great Mogul, but in the mute remorse and fear that follow upon his strange excesses, he is seized by an anguish known only to thieves and robbers on their way to the gallows. To put all this into words is nearly as rash as to try to read the thoughts of wild beasts. We can only hope to give a faint image of awesome and unspoken things.

The Gryla lives in Young Dunald's outhouse loft. Here she stays, in a dark space all the way up under the rafters. Only a single time each year does she come out to be among people and to have her big evening. The chamber where she lives cannot be entered from inside the building; the only entrance is a tiny door in the outside wall high up under the eaves, but that is sealed off with a heavy lock—and nailed up as well. Thus the Gryla's cage hangs between heaven and earth, pitch dark and cut off from the world like a raven's nest in the highest bluffs. Up there she broods all through the year, waiting for her hour to come, remote and hidden, though not forgotten. For who can forget the Gryla?

And yet when it comes to that, there is no one who can remember what she really looks like or who can describe her clearly. She is very shaggy and has horns and a tail. She gives off an unpleasant smell and utters queer sounds—some plaintive, some threatening, some quite indistinguishable—as if in a wild and agonized frenzy. Sometimes she sings as well, chanting old rhymes and dark refrains. Her face cannot be clearly discerned. It is large and very ugly but is hidden beneath a curtain of tatters and rags. There are many who have seen that her eyes shine in the dark, but this is about all that can be said for certain about her outward appearance. About her inner being nothing whatever is known, for her spirit is shrouded in mystery and rooted in the darkness of the primeval night.

Dunald is the only one who is on a personal footing with the Gryla. But the exact nature of his standing with her is hidden from the world. It is known that in moments of weakness he has been deeply unhappy about her and has called her a burden and a curse. And indeed, many people are greatly surprised that he has anything to do with her at all. In his daily comings and goings Dunald's manner is quiet and a bit shy, his speech is sad and dispirited, and his eyes are honest and melancholy. His whole demeanor makes people forget that he has anything to do with the Gryla. He is liked by everyone on the island. Helpful and trustworthy, he lends the farmers a good hand, particularly with any outdoor work—a great toiler. Since he is a poor man, nobody begrudges him what he gains from the Gryla. Nor does anyone try to pull his leg, for though he may not be a bright light, he is nobody's fool either. His memory is as good as anybody's, he knows as much as the next fellow about ancestry and family ties in the village, and he knows a number of old ballads. But in spite of all these good traits, Dunald is an odd character. He is not like other men. He is a loner and an outsider. All because of the Gryla.

It is the Monday before Lent, and Dunald feels a certain tension of body and soul that always comes at this time of year. His wife also notices his agitation. She sighs and stares into space, far from happy. This evening she has wept as she always does when she knows that Dunald has begun to potter about with the Gryla again. She knows that he is up in that ill-starred enclosure right now. She has heard him undoing the little door. She has heard the faint squeak of the nails being cautiously removed. But she has not been spying. That would be unbecoming of her, and it would do no good anyway. What must be, must be, just as it has been every year for the last fourteen and before that through endless years reaching back into the murky past. Before Young Dunald it was his father, Old Dunald, who had the Gryla, and before that again, *his* father.

Yes, Dunald is up in the cage. He is with the Gryla. In there it is as dark as inside a mouth. Yes, as within the jowl of a devilfish at the bottom of the sea. There is an overwhelming breath of mold, of dry rot, of wool and horn, and he sniffs this stuffy smell—sits for a long time savoring it, sore in spirit and with trembling heart at the thought of what is to come. Outside, the evening is soughing, the sea is breathing deeply and calmly, like time and eternity; the waves are breaking against the shore, and hollow, muffled groans are coming out of the grotto at Marragjógv. Dunald gropes around in the dark with greedy hands, moaning hoarsely. His excitement wells up in his throat and makes him lightheaded. Yes, it is all here—the fur and rags, the head, the bottle, and the *Great Peg.* It is all here the way he left it last year. It is all in order. And why shouldn't it be? There are no mice or rats on the island, no cats either, and thieves and pranksters most assuredly keep their distance. Dunald makes greedy movements in the darkness—in this mouth filled with all its teeth and tongues and uvulas—and wordlessly he says to himself: This is mine. The thought of all these treasures in here arouses him; he makes a silent grimace to himself in the darkness and solitude, he draws in his breath exuberantly, giving forth a faint palatal sound like that of a swooning woman. He feels that he is changing. The shape-changing will soon take place—has already begun.

Dunald can tell that his wife knows he has been with Gryla. She has been weeping. It is late evening, and the girls are asleep. Strange feelings are stirring within him, as always when *it* is about to happen. He is somewhat aloof from all the familiar things around him. A veil has been dropped between him and the everyday world. He begins to muse upon the wonder of it—that this should be his home—that this big woman Signa with her staring bird's eyes should be his wife. Strange to think that there are eight children already. Strange that they all should be girls, no sons—to be the only male among nine women. And strange to think, too, that shortly there will be lots of meat in the drying shed and in the cooking pot. The air already seems filled with the smell of this meat, both the dried and the cooked—but especially the cooked, with steam rising in yellow clouds that can almost be licked with the tongue. The tender dried meat, dark red and ash white, cut through with glassy seams of clear fat. And the strong, grayish yellow soup, which stings like a potion and seeps into every pore.

Signa steals a glance at him, a brief one, for it pains her; she feels a stab at her heart to see that the change has begun in Dunald, it is like alum in her soul and makes it shrivel. His eyes are small now and full of strange lights, his throat is numb with a passion that has nothing to do with her, he cannot hide his secret joy and excitement. Alas, if it only were over and done with. It is a thing that she must live through—this year as well.

It can be said of any holiday in the year that it has its proper meaning. Easter is the day of resurrection, bringing relief from the hardship of winter. Whitsun marks the beginning of summer, when the grass grows and mild voices are heard everywhere. Christmas is a great stirring in the darkness, joy and happiness, silver rays of hope rising from the depths of the year and reaching into every heart. But Shrovetide is profane—indeed, so unholy that many of the faithful will not see it as anything but a pagan curse and a cross to bear. In some villages it comes and goes unmarked—simply does not exist, as it were. But on the isle of Stapa its roots stubbornly stick in the barren soil and cannot be pulled out. The people here are on the whole no worse than in other places, or slower at learning, but in this one thing they go their own way. In short, they mark the approach of Lent in the spirit of their forefathers and in the way that their blood demands, when the soul is smitten with nameless pangs and a fire is lit that must burn itself out.

On the Monday before Lent there is dancing at one of the larger farms on the island. All but the sick and crippled take part, and there is eating and drinking till all hours. The feast is much like any other throughout the year, with one difference—one that everyone feels, even nowadays. There is a tiny but ominous loosening within the soul, a sweet seepage somewhere in the depths, a frolic in the darkness during which a single finger is teasingly reached out to the Devil. Older men take a drop more than they need, so that even the meekest do a little boasting and even the most silent become talkative. Young people are bolder than usual, and tempta-

tion lurks in every nook and loft. Afterward there is not only re-
morse but also relief, as always when compulsive deeds have been
done. There is no understanding this—that something which in
itself is unclean can bring about a cleansing—indeed, an uplifting.
It is as when the cow consumes all the unclean matter from her
newborn calf, making it clean and fresh by licking it with her
enormous rough tongue.

Ten or more years ago a movement against the Shrovetide feast
was started on the island, but it made no headway and lost its follow-
ing when it turned out that the missionary who was its spokesman
was a pervert and made love to little girls. And the Gryla, whom
this outsider had ranted against and attacked so bitterly that many
actually felt outraged on her behalf and Dunald's—the Gryla was
fully vindicated. Not to the extent that they began talking about
her and defending or praising her. The Gryla can't simply be dis-
cussed as if it were some unusual milch cow or stallion. She does
not lend herself to the spoken word, she is no human being with
virtues and faults, she is simply the Gryla—for better or for worse.
She has her comings and her goings, and that is all.

She has her coming on Tuesday evening when the merrymakers
have frolicked to the point of weariness, when they are sore of
limb and soul and the Devil is standing behind them counting col-
lected fingers in the dark shadow of their deeds. Then her time is
at hand. It is then that she has her coming.

She is back again. No one has seen her come down from
Dunald's loft, no one knows from which corner of the world she
has come. Some boys claim to have seen her stealing up from
Marragjógv. Anyway, she has come. She walks in the moonless
twilight, she strides, short and broad, through the muddy farm-
yards, she lifts and lowers her horned head, she makes cuddlesome
sounds with the voice of an infant, she laughs and chuckles with
the deep voice of a man. She is huge, much like a stack of peat, she
drags a long, rustling tail behind her, it rattles and bumps like
empty pots and kettles, this tail—busily dinning like a whole
smithy of dwarfs. Now and then the Gryla stops, played out,
stretching herself full length with her snout to the ground, much
like a tussock among other tussocks. At times she lifts her head
high and sniffs the drizzly darkness, or she twists and turns and
treads a slow dance on one spot. Or she sets off at a run in clumsy
leaps, acting like a stir-crazy cow.

There are only half-grown lads trailing behind the Gryla. The girls hang back, not to mention the smaller children, who at most make bold to peek at the Gryla from windows and alleyways. Even the biggest louts are for the most part not very forward. Only one person in all her following undertakes anything that makes him stand out in any way, and that is Óli "Hekk," a little man of ripe age who is a bit weak-minded. At happenings like this he is in high spirits, shouting and waggling so that no one can say whether he is angry or just wildly happy. Óli Hekk has a lifeless tongue, and all he can say is *hekk,* which accounts for his nickname. Óli's constant *hekk*'ing gives people a way of knowing where the Gryla is at any given time. Her progress around the village is wavering and whimsical, she does not go from one door to the next but makes large sweeps hither and yon, straying into the fields, disappearing among the rocks by the stream, turning back to the houses again, sticking her nose in at some doorway and standing there perhaps briefly, perhaps for quite some time.

At some doorways she stays longer than usual, seemingly busy with something or other. Once in a while she comes all the way in to linger in a kitchen or in a living room. In some rare cases she may be turned away, and then she will back off, but in most places she is welcomed and given her gifts: bread, cakes, brandy, here and there a coin, but for the most part dried mutton—shoulder, shank, or rib—which is handed in to her underneath the steaming fur. Where she knows that it will be taken in the right spirit, she exposes the Great Peg, and it is a sight to behold—enormous and realistic. Of course not everybody has laid eyes on it; nevertheless it is remarkable how many will tolerate the sight and freely say so—not only men but womenfolk as well. Indeed, even old women take no offense at it by any means. The oldest islanders can recall earlier times, or at least tales of earlier times, when there was more to this night than merely accepting the Great Peg—when the very sight of it was thought to be a blessing to any household and it was an evil omen if it did not show itself or if the Gryla passed by. Young women whose marriage was without blessing were healed if the Peg touched their naked flesh underneath their skirts. And other kinds of fruitfulness were also believed to be furthered by the Gryla—that of the animals of the farm and that of the soil itself. She could even bring about good fishing. People's belief in these powers has no doubt grown weaker since that time, but it is not altogether gone. It dwells on quietly in many minds, even among those who are unaware of it.

But what about Dunald himself?

Very few can conceive of what he goes through in the course of the Gryla's rounds. It takes the strength of a horse to bear her enormous weight and to endure the heat and the lack of air under the heavy furs and vestments, at the same time doing the long and involved work of the Gryla. Dunald has this strength even though he is a weak and ungifted person in his daily life. He will go through it all triumphantly now as so often in the past, and the way his fathers did before him. The rare gifts that have been handed down to him are the strength of the artist at play and the endurance of the priest at his devotions. As he moves about here in the darkness of the barren island he is the spokesman of life. Heathen, yes. But not the Anti-Christ that the carping missionary would make him. He is the Anti-Death. All know this, but without openly admitting it. For this reason joy and delight attend the Gryla, but with a certain amount of shyness. For the Devil with his bundle of collected fingers is ever nearby, and whatever they may feel about the Gryla, none would go so far as to say that she is fair in the sight of God. God and the Gryla are incompatible, cannot be harbored within the same thought. They are two forces like fire and water. There is a seething and darkening where they meet, and therefore they are kept strictly apart. Shrove Tuesday has no God. It has the Gryla. Once in the dim past the Gryla was all-powerful. Though no one can remember it, vague memories of it course through the blood as deep-sea fish do along the ocean bottom. Assuredly, God's is the power over all things, yet there is one evening out of the hundreds in the year that the Gryla can call her own.

But this is not Dunald's way of thinking. His thoughts are not clothed in fine words. They are age-old springs gushing up in his spirit. They are as formless as dreams—as fire and water—as snowy clouds or swirling streams in the sea. They uplift him and enable him to bear the monstrous burden that gnaws and scratches at his back till the sweat runs in thick streams and the steam of his body blocks the breathing-holes of the mask.

Strange, nameless, and everlasting forces are at work within Dunald, making him strong and light-footed, filling him with a high and self-righteous kind of abandon—making it a good thing to be a snail within this rough shell.

He grasps the Great Peg. It gives him a dizzy feeling of power to have this borer with him, this penetrant, this marvelous implement of preservation and regeneration. Do not belittle the power of the Great Peg! It must play its part if the fishing is to be as good this spring as last. It can keep April frosts from harming the newborn lambs and from taking their toll of the sheep the way they did last year. It can soften the spring drought that often comes with the east winds and slows the sprouting, and it can hold back the autumn rains that turn the hay to slime and cut down the size of the herds. It will bless the seed in the soil and in the womb. It was made for luck and happiness, for the wonders and the many joys of creation in bed, in the stable, in nests, and all the breeding places of the sea and the cliffs. It exists to uphold life in all things.

Old and wordless songs of praise, deep and unfathomable, lurk in Dunald's soul. He cannot understand them, but their forces sing within him languidly like great, swirling waters under the new moon, now that he is at the height of his powers and is fulfilling his life's calling. Great is the fruitfulness of the Gryla. She will put great things in motion. She is cow and bull, mare and stallion, she is akin to the milky spawning-waters of the fishing banks and the green and darkling places that surround the whales in their mating under distant skies. She knows the blackness where waxing and waning meet and all rises from nothing. She is the wild stream of sperm when it thrusts itself like a powerful shooting star into the deluvian darkness, letting life win over death. . . .

Thus does power sing within Dunald in dizzy moments, but his exuberance is not unflagging. There are times when doubt and fatigue wash over him in heavy seas and crushing waves, and his pace must slacken. Then it is that the Gryla throws herself down and becomes as nothing in the dark; then it is that the man within her feels frightened and miserable like Jonah in the whale, and he must force the bitter brandy down even though he never takes a drop in daily life. It is not done without anguish; he often retches, giving up gall and shedding salty tears, but relief and balm soon come to him and the joy of living rushes back. He peers out through the Gryla's nostrils, which are his eyes. He recovers himself, gets up and moves on.

"Hekk!"

The broken word sounds forth like a battle cry from Óli, who never for a moment has left the Gryla's side.

There are only seventeen houses in the village on the isle of Stapa, and by midnight the Gryla has just about ended her rounds. There still remains the finale, the great last dance that is the crowning event in her visitations and that takes place in the middle of the village, on the site of a burnt-down house where an open square has been left.

The great dance of the Gryla is signaled by fresh *hekk* cries of renewed vigor, and a feverish stir arises in the crowd of half-grown boys. There are scoldings and whinings as the youngest louts get pulled out and marched home by grim-faced mothers. There remain then the wiliest and boldest of them, and these are joined by a few grownups—not from the best circles. At this point there are not many windows showing light, the houses loom dark and dead with their grassy roofs bristling against the veil of northern lights in the sky beyond the sea. But something is stirring in a window here and there, and alleyways and crannies seem to be full of faces. The darkness in Dunald's little house, however, is no sham; it is deadly earnest. Shame and sorrow hold sway here, the wife and daughters have gone to bed, and the youngest ones are asleep. Signa and the two eldest are lying awake, and the darkness in the cramped bedchamber is filled with restless sighing. In Signa's spirit night reigns supreme, she has armed her heart with bitterness, frost has found its way into her soul.

Outside on the open square the thing has happened which always happens: the Gryla has gone wild, she tumbles tramping hither and yon, chanting voices clamor inside her as of many men in the chain dance,* and the tail clatters deafeningly. And lo, suddenly she raises the part in front like a rutting stallion and gives forth a neigh so forceful and real that it goes to the very marrow—an inhuman masterpiece of sound that no one who has heard it can ever forget. And in the growing northern lights the Great Peg can

---

* The unique Faroese dance, performed by men and women or by men alone, side by side in a moving ring formed by interlocked arms. The simple tramping steps are accompanied by ancient, chanted ballads. This dance has been handed down from the Middle Ages and is still very popular in the islands.—H.B.

be seen, exposed and in daring movement. Rearing mightily the monster turns, like a bell of darkness with the clapper free and swinging, the rarest of sights, a revelation so amazing that the onlooker can do nothing but gape. The houses are wide-eyed, the black windowpanes stare, eyes seem to be present in all corners, behind curtains and at half-open doors, and Óli forgets his cries. In the great stillness of the night nothing can be heard but the passionate and frightening cascades of animal sounds that lustfully pour from the lifted jowl of the Gryla.

Then the great body sinks down again, stretches itself flat and seems sunk into the ground. So lies the Gryla for a while. Those who are standing nearest can hear her unearthly groaning, which little by little gives way to an agonized cough and a choked and helpless cry of anguish.

Then she rises once more, and now the way turns homeward, for now her time is past. She has lost all her spirit. Limp and wobbling she goes off into the darkness, and now she is to be left alone. No one must follow her those last steps to her well-earned rest. Even Óli Hekk knows this. He stands back silently, wiping the sweat from his brow. He too has had a trying evening.

For Dunald there now remains the aftermath, to which there is both a blissful side and a grim one.

The evening's efforts have been devastating to Dunald, wearing him to his utmost limits. But as soon as he has reached his home and has pulled off the dripping-wet burden and thrown it on the stone floor of the outhouse, his weariness leaves him, put to flight by his anguish. For some moments the bitter saliva runs and he swallows hard, weeping like a child. No being in all the world needs comforting now as Dunald does—and sympathy and understanding. From being the center of every one's attention he has suddenly sunk to being the loneliest creature on the island, a scapegoat, a weakling, a wretch, a leper. He is hungry and thirsty in body and soul, dirty, besmirched, and damned, without friends, without family. For there is no use going to Signa and trying to soften her heart—he knows that from bitter experience. She has shut herself off within a shell of frost; she will avoid him for weeks, and her daughters too. Even the little ones she will mercilessly keep away from him. Food will be denied him. He will have to stay in the Gryla's cage, lying there in cold and darkness, shriveled within the loneliness of remorse and despair. And for the time being he will not dare to face other people either; it will take time and a great effort to struggle back to life and reality from the world of the Gryla.

But this is not the worst of it. The worst is that he may not cry to God and seek the comfort of Heaven. Not that anybody has taken Dunald aside and told him so. No, it is something that he knows and always has known, and that all men know: there are certain things that do not concern the Almighty and have no place in his solemn scheme. But these are the very things that belong in the realm of Beelzebub, and he is always on hand to claim his due. Alas, he is so close that the air is filled with his smell—the smell of goat and scorched horn.

That is the nature of Dunald's suffering. That is the price he must pay, there is no other way, cold terror shows its unrelenting face, and there is nothing to do but yield to it and endure the pains that await him.

But before he submits to the yoke he will once more find comfort and will pluck from this night yet another strange and delightful fruit. It is the thought of this fruit that makes the burden of gloom and remorse bearable and casts such a glow that all is not despair and darkness after all.

Dunald pulls himself together with a sigh and begins to pick the Gryla gifts out of the heap on the floor. Hangs up the meat. Puts things in order. But right in the middle of it all, he is again overcome with fatigue and pain and can do no more. Sparks and fiery flowers burst out of the darkness around him, and arousing visions take shape in his mind—sea anemones and other creatures of the deep. Yes, the time has come—he must go now—the fruit must be plucked and the thirst quenched.

Dunald's nocturnal visit to Isan will not be narrated in any detail here; it will merely be briefly recounted in the interest of fairness and accuracy. Isan—or Elisabeth, as her real name is—lives by herself but does not lead the shy and retiring life that one might think. On the contrary, few women on Stapa get around to as many places as Isan or are as sought after and esteemed. She cooks and helps at weddings and funerals, she assists the midwife at nearly all deliveries, she has no mean ability as a healer and knows remedies for many ailments, and she is not sparing of her help. Of all living things on the island, she is the only one that understands Dunald's distress in this night and knows how to relieve it and bring the harried man comfort in his need.

First she cooks a nourishing meal, which includes among other things a mild herb soup and two raw egg yolks. All is peace and quiet while this is being done; there is no asking or prying, no exchange of disturbing words. A kind of solemnity reigns at the table here in Isan's cozy and well-kept room; it is like the eve of a holiday, and Isan herself is wearing a Sunday dress with a freshly ironed, flowery apron. A fire is crackling in the stove and the pendulum of the wall clock is moving back and forth with polite little clicks in the stillness.

While Dunald is eating Isan is in the kitchen making things ready for the cleansing. A mild fragrance of soap and steaming water blends with the smell of coffee. Bed sheets are being warmed and clean towels laid out. After the washing, which takes several changes of water and cannot be done without Isan's help, Dunald lies down to rest, clean and fresh, and watches while Isan scrubs and rinses his soiled clothes and hangs them up to dry. Isan is a little woman with good color in her face and very quick blue eyes. She is a bit over forty and has been a widow for fifteen years— that is, if widow is the right word, for nobody really knows whether her husband is living. He was a strange and callous man, violent-tempered and much given to drink, and life was far from pleasant for Isan while they were living together. But he left her and went to Nordvik on Husoy, where he lived with another woman. Later he abandoned this mistress as well and left the country. But enough of him. He isn't worth remembering, and no one misses him—least of all Isan.

Lying here in Isan's bed with its fragrance of clean sheets, Dunald feels almost as if he were transported to the days of his earliest childhood. Pleasant daydreams sail by in his mind, the events of the evening fade away, all memories are gently rocked to sleep in a surge of forgetfulness, the moment unfolds like some rare and heavenly flower—the only one of its kind. Once more Dunald is overcome by his feelings. But in the midst of all this joy there is a little cold spot, an aching grain of unhappiness. Only a grain as yet, but it will sprout and quickly send forth great leaves spreading a dark shadow of distress. As long as the seed grain remains sleeping in its soil, however, his joy is like a miracle.

The light is put out. For a brief moment dread and dismay again wrap their dark wings around him. But then Isan comes to him, silent and calm, with burning cheeks.

In the early light of dawn Dunald goes down to the shore. Here he stands staring out across the open sea for yet a while before he goes home to penitence in the Gryla's lair high up in the dark loft.

SIX POEMS

DAVID GIANNINI

For Fran

DRAWING NEAR YOUR HOUSE

I have taken from its place
water that knows
the lives of stone.

Our hill creek lips close
around water
that takes
the shape of us within.

I have borne many reasons
for loving you,
your body of the moon,
but none so simple
as water taken
from its place among stone.

IMAGES OF AFTERNOON

Working in red shade, shade of opened plants and clothing, I see
the ants
are also busy, licking the sweet juices from locked peonies.

Breezes, the sun rocked low. The shovel and the spade overturn
less,
the shadow of the bee is no longer cast, across columbine and tulips.

By tumbrel I push weed and tuckahoe to death's mound, set tools,
ease through
timothy so tall it touches the lips of a man walking.

Now the barn windows drift with more shade, the duck eggs and
feathers must
be quiet as beams, letting the floor hay stretch, frail, useful, stained.

I will eat thinking of first things, and of the thrush surprised in its
nest
under the spires of blue rye, under the spittlebug's harvest.

Eyes closed, I open the dark inside. White flowers with black notes
clinging,
the hum of things coming forward, the iron sun, train coming
forward bearing our own blood.

NEAR THE PETERSBURG PASS

Here, pine crosses
with porcelain terminals
hold raspberry vine
upon vine, dark
eyes buds
insect & unopen.

Beyond them
bobcat yells
split a hill
& the whole cedar
cat-shocked dusk
kneels on last wires

of light—wild
feline running
spirit between dells
aching out
of throat
the first killed

silence of world.

"ARCHIE"

Because the face of this farmer
resembles the seven mountains
around him—the cut-rock
head, the turning boulder
on the poplar-necked hill—
these grasses, birds, even
the whole and foxy weather
come easy come hard to him
as rain with its hard-soft hits
wrinkles, drills the spring
field with its future in wheat . . .
I praise his face with its seven mountains.

THE BARN

Today, even the hawk stays
gripping the wing-fold tree;
wind rips the heads of flowers;
I hear the wind in my skull
dismantling me. I can hear it
my skull creak like a weak barn,
the hoofs of startled animals inside
knocking at their stalls. I walk
into a barn disguised as a barn, sprawl
on straw and cannot move, cannot move.
I hear the dark stir of their shoes
stamp in the locked weather
of the barn. I am the barn and cannot move:
I am the place of dark animals.
When the youngest mare among them breaks
free, I crack under her accurate hoofs.

POEM

A lake
the color of deep fern
and after
swimming you shake off
its seed;
after your moist strip
you pull through the placket
of your dress
and the sun of it
settles,

your face with the under hue
of peeled birch
rubbed with an oil.

The slim
canoe of your voice
the strong
red woman up front
glide through a choice of shade.

A shadow
the texture of star moss
and lightly
you slip off your dress
its wrinkled sun
on a tom-thumb lawn.
Your breasts without tan
I moisten
your dark inland
I open,

feel where the lake brushed
kiss
where the lake washed

the damp
walls around the warming pool
the wet stone
swelling and
hold (hold) come around me now.

THREE POEMS

GUSTAF SOBIN

TROUBADOUR

what I love's the
squander, to
spend
and spend, through the
cold air 'run

with the pennants,' as if
world

were still
to be reached, wrung from its
mirrors: wind, gypsum,
brushweed,
all

those des-
olate metals. its
'meanings'
breached, blown

through . . . you'd

turned
to a distance. in-

to you (the skirt, the
pearl of
your skirt spreading, like a *resonance,*
an *element*) I'd risen.
routes

of Provence, smoke
in drafts through the black cypresses. . . .
'there's this, this,' you
tell me. as the

fingers open, they're
filling
with curls.

SHADOW RATTLES

1

  what the eye flies after trans-
    luces; what
you want, doesn't want: it vanishes. . . .

  you're only yours, mutter and
muscles, as you enter it, its vanishing.

2

sound, too (the cricket ticking
in dry grass) cracks light. 'out, out, out,'
you'd written,
your only
where.

3

(Simiane-la-Rotonde)

in bowls
of glowing wind, bristles   violet. look,
how you
look, turn   thirsting towards. but
already, in the

breath-
beaten mirrors, the stacked lavender burns.

4

      then, suddenly, you stood there and
             I couldn't
believe it. I pretended it was you, and that

you stood there, and was me that you gazed at.

5

mirror-
less except for this: those   gray eyes, their
        quick slip   sideways. . . .

6

draws us, that
dim
    residual pearl (anywhere, would go   anywhere
to reach it,
to dissolve in that   light that's outside of us).

7

nothing, finally,
was worthier than the grief that forced the question,
the earth-
hooded worder   forwards.

8

light again, and then
gone. in the
wobbling
word-
pitted hollow (writing, you said,
that you wouldn't
be written) the
real, un-
remittent grace of the impossible.

THUS

from there, the
wave's

tiny,
ruffled, like
a doll's sleeve. we're
feeding

on so little, sip-
ping breath
out of

whispers, signs, the
story that's
hidden, em-
bedded, in another (*'can't*

*be told, can
never. . . .'*). but

glints
through the twin windows,
ripples

gold
where the mouth, once,

broke open.

CLEARING IN THE FOREST

A short play

JAMES PURDY

GIL. I don't know why you wanted to invite her to supper, then, since all you've done all afternoon is run her down!

BURK. Aren't you going to marry her?

GIL. Well, what if I am.

BURK. You mean you don't know yet!

GIL. Burk, you confuse me so! Of course I'm going to marry her if you'll let both of us alone.

BURK. I let both of you alone! Hear him! You two haven't left me alone have you?

GIL. But, Burk, you wanted to loan us the money. And we paid most of it back already . . . And we'll pay all of it back . . . Burk, you shouldn't have gone and cooked this big meal for us tonight. You know it always makes you nervous . . . And she doesn't know the first thing about good cooking in any case . . . Burk, are you listening.

BURK. Yes, Burk's listening. Listening good. (*He goes back into the kitchen section and stirs something in a heavy kettle.*) This will be a farewell dinner, you might say.

GIL. I wish you wouldn't talk like that . . . Even after we're married we'll be close friends.

BURK (*coming forward*). I never want to see you again, or her, after you're married. Is that clear?

GIL (*imploring, hurt*). Burk, you can't mean a thing . . . that terrible.

BURK. Oh, can't I. You don't know Burk then.

GIL. All these two years we've lived together taught me that . . . You are always different, like the sea. Only you're not like the sea either . . . You can always see it whatever it's mood.

BURK. Oh, the sea, the sea. You always talk about it because you never set eyes on it before you came to live with me.

GIL. Burk, I don't regret . . . our friendship . . .

BURK (*stung*). Oh, it's friendship now, is it . . . Well, marry your girl friend and forget we ever met . . .

GIL. I wish you wouldn't of invited her here tonight . . . I feel I can't go through with it. (*Throws himself down on a dilapidated davenport.*)

BURK. Gil, what's wrong?

GIL. *What's wrong* he asks . . . I bet when your ocean drowns a hundred people and holds them down there in his special locker, he wonders why they don't talk back to him anymore! *What's wrong?* Everything's wrong, and always has been.

BURK. Well don't ever say I stood in the way of your getting married to Louise . . . You can't hang that one on me too . . .

GIL. *Too!* Well, what else do I hang on you! Huh?

BURK. Let me tell you, you have been a drag on me, Gil Stockton! Since the day you arrived here without even a decent pair of shoes on your big feet, you have drained me dry!

GIL. And I never give you nothin' in return either, did I?

BURK (*ashamed*). We'll go into that in the next world . . .

GIL. I'll count on it.

BURK. Well, why do you think I'm going to all this bother of a eight course dinner if I don't think you give me something!

GIL. But it's the wrong kind of thank you, Burk . . . It makes me feel, like you always make me feel, indebted . . . and guilty!

BURK. Well, you ought to feel some indebtedness to me, shouldn't you . . . As to guilty, you'll have to take that up with your preacher.

GIL. You're my preacher!!! (*Said in rage and passion.*)

BURK. Oh, don't hang that on me too.

GIL. You're him, you're my mother, my father, my brother, my scold . . . You might as well be my wife! (*He breaks down.*)

BURK (*despite Gil's collapse, fierce*). Look here, Goldylocks, don't you ever call me a wife again (*Pointing to a huge meat fork*) or this goes right through your little windpipe . . . Nobody ever even suggested when I was in the navy for six years and in combat and after that the Merchant Marine, see, nobody ever suggested I had that (*Snaps his fingers*) of the cunt in me . . . Do you hear?

GIL. Then if you're so much a man, why do you have to give this long speech about it.

BURK. Your wife! Shit.

GIL. Oh come off it . . . Nobody ever thought you were anybody's wife . . . Just because you cook so good, and look so nice . . .

BURK. Look so nice! I don't look so nice any more after all the years of taking care of you . . . God damn it to hell, now you made me burn the sauce. (*Rushes over to the stove.*)

GIL. Boy, oh boy, who will you have to blame when I am a married man. Who will get it in the neck then I wonder. Do you like Louise just a little bit, Burk . . . I want you to like her.

BURK. Do I have to cook and also praise your bride at the same time?

GIL. You only have to answer one little question . . .

BURK (*growls it*). No.

GIL (*suddenly with passion*). Just tell me you like her a little bit even if you don't . . . Burk . . . (*Goes over to him . . . they look at one another then suddenly fall into one another's arms.*)

BURK (*disentangling himself, suddenly*). If you want me to say I love her or adore her or whatever, I will for you . . . I want you to be happy. After all, what future have you got here . . .

GIL. But I'd like you to mean it, Burk . . . I can't bear the thought of giving you . . . up . . . after we're married and all . . .

BURK. How can I like her, Gil? I mean . . . (*He turns away.*)

GIL (*musing*). You couldn't even, maybe, pretend to like her.

BURK (*in another outburst*). You know me . . . I never can keep down anything I feel . . . That was why I was in so much trouble in the navy . . . Always in hot water for not kissing some

little ensign or lieutenant's or commander's ass . . . They would
have kept me in irons for my whole service if they could have . . .
And I feel that way now, and always have, Gil . . . You've kept
me in irons! And now after having chained me till I'm no good for
any other human being, down in the brig where you've kept me,
you're going off with this . . . cunt! (*Turns away in a paroxysm
of rage.*)

GIL. Burk, if you only knew what this does to me inside . . . It's
. . . (*Sobs*) . . . killing me.

BURK. Killing you! (*Said maniacally.*)

GIL. The fact is (*Barely controlling himself*) I don't see how I
can do without you once I am married . . . I mean, what is
Louise, after all . . .

BURK. One flesh with you . . . That's what she will be when
you're married. And you won't and can't and shan't have me and
you know it . . . Louise won't have me! You know that . . .
Even for supper once a month would be too much for her . . . Do
you know how she looks at me when I am looking at you . . . Do
you! Answer me, God damn you, do you know how she looks at
me when I am looking at you? (*Takes hold of Gil with mania.*)
Tell me how . . .

GIL. Burk, you're choking the daylights out of me . . . Let go,
let go. (*He turns away.*)

BURK. You tell me how she looks at me then! Do you hear, God
damn you!

GIL. Burk, you're . . . breaking me . . . Don't you see . . .
Burk. (*He falls to his knees.*) Burk, I love you the most, you know
that, but you're breaking me.

BURK. You tell me how she looks at me when I am looking at
you!

GIL (*as if mesmerized, and still on his knees*). She looks at you
as if she could tear you limb from limb . . . She looks at you like
a famished . . . tiger . . . that hadn't no food . . .

(*Burk flings Gil to the floor so that he lies prone, sobbing.*)

BURK. And I'm cooking this fucking feast for her!

GIL. I'll call her, Burk. We'll cancel it . . . We'll not have . . .
the feast.

BURK. We'll have it, God damn it, if I have to shove all eight courses down both your craws! Is that clear? We'll have the feast! And we'll like it.

GIL. Burk, look what you're doing to me . . . Look how I'm trembling . . . Look at me!

BURK (*coming over close to him*). If you could see into my guts, my heart and bowels and kidney and bladder and spleen and all the vessels that guide and prompt my cock too . . . if you could see what you have done over the years to all the man inside of me . . . and you complain about your fucking little trembling fingers. (*Strikes him.*) You've destroyed me! (*Goes back into kitchen area and flings himself down in a wooden chair.*)

GIL (*turns as if to the audience*). Destroyed him . . . Oh, God . . . I feel my brain has turned . . . (*Pauses*) Burk, we have destroyed one another then . . . I told you the truth a moment ago . . . I love only you . . . I don't know how or why . . . I've heard of boys (*As if to himself*) who loved the storm even after they had been struck and singed by the lightning and drowned by the rain and deafened by the thunder . . . When the great summer thundershowers would be at their height whether in the dead of night, or before the dawn had come, they would steal out of their warm beds, and go into the clearing before the forest, and look up into the wild eye of the tempest, they would hold their body and soul up to its destruction, not just once in a lifetime, but again, again, again! (*He falls down on his knees and covers his face with his hands.*)

BURK. But you are a deserter. (*Said with real madness.*)

(*Gil shakes his head as he holds it with his hands.*)

Do you hear what I say to you.

GIL. Don't say it . . . Certain things should not be said!

BURK (*rising and coming over to him*). You deserted . . . your lightning, your storm.

GIL. Don't touch me . . . I can't bear it right now.

BURK (*putting on a gold-colored jacket*). I will never touch you again . . . She shall touch you . . . forever and ever until death do you part . . .

GIL. Don't say that.

BURK. You can say anything to a deserter.

GIL. Don't call me that, I can't bear it.

BURK. What shall I call you then.

GIL (*standing up and going over to Burk, but with considerable distance still between them*). Don't call me that name.

BURK. What name should I use for you then, if *deserter's* not to be spoke.

GIL. Couldn't you call me the one that loved you the most.

BURK. No . . . He died. He's dead to me even now . . .

GIL. Then I can't bear that! Burk, listen to me . . . I can't go on living without your . . . caring . . . and seeing me . . . and being with me . . . Don't you understand . . . Louise could be nothing to me the way you are.

BURK. But you only need the lightning and the tempest . . . when there is a storm . . . On the quiet and the good nights you will sleep with her, is that it? And be happy! And have children, and the rest . . . But when you are you, and the sea and earth rise up in battle and clash, you will want to come with me . . . For the quiet won't be enough.

GIL (*as if stunned, or having drunk a narcotic*). Something like that . . .

BURK. But what if there are no more storms, no waking in the night and rushing out to the clearing in the forest where the lightning and thunder and the riven trees fall to the ground, what if there is only the quiet of the womb, and the bed where children are made endlessly in soft comforters and sheets . . .

GIL. Then I'll die, Burk.

BURK (*taking him*). Renounce her, take me . . .

GIL. I can't stand a life . . . either . . . of all storms and flashes of lightning . . .

(*Burk, overcome by his feelings, embraces Gil deliriously.*)

What are you doing to me now . . . ?

BURK. What does it matter . . .

GIL. You've forgotten the . . . feast?

BURK. I've forgotten everything . . .

GIL. Burk, Burk.

BURK. What is it?

GIL. Am I all right, Burk.

BURK. What do you mean, dear boy. Aren't you in my arms.

GIL. Burk, I am not myself . . . Listen . . . When you made that speech . . .

BURK. You have nothing to worry about . . .

GIL. When you made that speech . . . about the clearing in the forest, the storm, the sky that falls to the earth and so on . . . Burk! Something broke in my brain . . . I am not trying to frighten you. Something broke . . . Maybe a blood vessel . . . Burk, I am not Gil anymore . . . You must call Louise and tell her not to come . . .

BURK. No, no, that is quite out of the question . . . Contrary to what you think, I have everything prepared . . . Don't you know I am a master chef, Gil.

GIL. You are everything, and everybody I have ever hoped to know and love . . . You are my all, Burk.

BURK. You are tired, my dear boy . . . I think you must go into the next room for a little rest. Lie down on our bed, and I will call you when supper is ready. Do you hear . . . (*Kisses him.*) You should not worry about the supper though . . . It will be a feast, as I said before . . . A feast fit for a queen like Louise! (*He laughs but Gil does not respond . . . He stares at him, begins to see something terrible has gone wrong.*) Gil, dear heart, you shall marry Louise, if you like . . . And I will visit the both of you . . . Gil, Gil. (*Holds him to him.*) You shall have both her . . . and the lightning . . . Gil, what is it?

(*The doorbell rings in loud terrible peremptoriness.*)

(*Rising.*) That must be her now . . . Do you hear, Gil? I wish you would go into the next room and lie down . . . on . . . the bed. Can't I help you. Gil!

GIL (*with terrible loudness*). Leave me alone . . . Leave me here . . . near you . . . I don't want to leave the room without you . . . Leave me here, Burk . . . Where are you?

BURK (*takes his hand*). I just said Louise is ringing the bell and I will go down now and let her in . . . We will have our . . . wedding supper then . . . (*He kisses Gil on the forehead, but stands a long time gazing at him with deep worry, then goes out.*)

GIL (*alone*). There will be no wedding supper, and there will be no wedding. There will be no warm nights with comforters and sheets in which I will lie against Louise's womb, and father her children, and the children will not sleep with us in warm comforters . . . My mother always said and I did not know what she meant, *Little Gil was struck by lightning when a child, and it has*

*made him love the storm and the wind and the thunder and to be
alone in the forest.*

*(He goes over to the kitchen and takes out a great extremely
thin and very long knife, and brings it back to face the audience.)*

*(Showing the knife, which flashes:) Little Gil looks into the very
face of the lightning whereas we and the rest of the children al-
ways ran and hid in darkness.*

*(He stabs himself vehemently again and again.) Little Gil was
never afraid of the forked, the cerise, the red, or the silver light-
ning . . . They flashed no fear into his mind.*

(Stabs himself again and again)

BURK *(enters).* Louise will be up in just a moment. *(He does
not notice Gil at first who has fallen facing the audience on the
floor.)* Gil? She is . . . *(He sees him.)* . . . up the . . . long
stairs . . . which have made her out of breath . . . *(Rushes
back to the door and slams it against Louise's entry.)* Gil! Oh God!
Gil, what have you done. *(He takes the knife out of his hands and
throws it away from them.)* Gil, for God in heaven . . .

GIL. I could not live without the lightning, Burk, or you . . .
(He kisses him.)

BURK. But what about the lightning, did you ever think about
that, Gil . . . What about it?

GIL. What about it?

BURK. Who will see the lightning, Gil, now in the clearing in the
forest?

*(Gil falls against Burk and dies . . . Burk holds him to him
. . . the doorbell rings loudly and desperately.)*

BARRACK GERMANY

HORST BIENEK

Translated from the German by Ralph Read

O Germany, still pale Mother,
in your womb I do not feel sheltered,
yet I wish it were otherwise,
but three times already you have cast me out;
again and again I have sought refuge
in your *house;* now we have built it anew
and many are those who helped us do so,
but I do not delude myself, it is temporary:
a *barracks*—how long will it endure?
And you sit inside, Janus-headed, gazing to the East
and the West, among the peoples
you still strike them as strange.
I admit it: I do not trust you.
(Only in your language do I feel at home.)

Three times already I have moved
from one Germany to the other.
In 1921 a piece of Silesia in which
my parents lived was lost
after bloody revolts. Now Polish was spoken.

So they moved westward across the river
to Gleiwitz, where I was born,
on the banks of the Klodnitz, which they still called
(tenderly) the Klodka. And one day
our street was renamed, Pruske Street
became Schlageter Street, and the *Square of the Republic*
became the Square of the S. A.   And in the same year
the synagogue on Niederwall Street burned.
On Good Friday of 1943, they took the last Jews
from their communal home
and dragged them to Auschwitz,
no farther than fifty km. away.
O Germany, pale Mother.

In January of '45, as the Stalin organ was howling
above the town, the train of refugees straggled
toward the Oder, ice cracking on their eyelashes,
it was so cold, the railroads already bombed.
Pattas, the priest who had hidden so long:
Listen to God's words again, and mine;
turn back and remain in your homes, your
homeland is here and your language, and so we remained,
chewing a few morsels of Polish: *moj Boze kochana.*

But then came the scourgers, who themselves
had been scourged, from Lemberg,
and, with a ten kilo bundle on my back, I moved
toward the West, where German was spoken,
and chance spat me out in Cöthen,
where Bach had once composed the Well-Tempered Clavier
and the Brandenburg Concertos,
here I lived in Barrack Germany,
and the wind blew its way through me.
Then in Berlin I learned the Organon
of the Epic Theater, read Kafka and Faulkner
secretly and smuggled texts to my friends
about the God who was none, wrote about
having and not having and as a boy
cried with Perrudja, an angel looking homewards,

and had enough of wars,
of Carthage the Great . . .
O Germany, pale Mother.

Then they came for me and interrogated me
under a spotlight, and on their caps
the Red Star burned, and they took me
eastward, as far as anyone could imagine,
to Vorkuta, Taischet, and Novosibirsk,
the endless Gulag Archipelago, where
—do not forget it!—
there is room for the entire West. And yet,
four years later, I was westward bound again,
with cap and pea-jacket, but free—
to Frankfurt, to Cologne and to Munich.
No Bienek had yet come so far.
And for the third time into a different Germany,
Barrack Germany, and I learned my lesson,
Germany, pale Mother. Yes, I learned . . .

Saw the people in the Oktoberfest tent, a people of underlings
where one half of them lies in wait to put
the other half behind barbed wire . . . A fright,
a vision, a nightmare?
Where like in the Wild West
a bounty is set on the heads of the hunted;
once it was Goerdeler, and a simple
peasant woman received 100,000 Reichsmarks.
I still remember, I
was a child at the time. What may have become of her?
Would not that be fine material, describing such a life?
And who will denounce whom today?
For the inflationary mark?
And whom will that bring death, and whom misfortune?

Must then the persecuted become
the persecutors one day and the persecutors
the persecuted? O Germany, pale Mother,
will I have to move even farther west some day

so as not to sit befouled among peoples
and not to stand out among the besmirched?
I hope that of your sons none more lie slain.

Hunger will be no more
and no one will raise his hand against his brother.
There shall be peace in your bisected Barracks,
no more marching and no *weapons* drill
for children, and will the lies fall silent
and the truth be printed, there too?
O Germany, uncanny Mother.

All around the rich praise you,
but the poor accuse you,
they point their fingers at you,
for you could do more for them.
The industrial nations, to be sure, extol
the system which was devised in your house
and elsewhere.
And yet they all see you conceal the hem
of your skirt which is bloody.
From the blood of others, yes, and also
from the blood of your own sons. Do not forget that.
Woe, it has not been so long ago.

"I love my country. I love
my people. I love my homeland." Chekhov.
Why do such sentences pass my lips
only as quotations?

Listening to the speeches that swell out
from your Barracks, one should reflect, even outside.
Some things have changed. Even more will change.
We will not allow
what has already happened once
to happen again.

I will have to do something about that, pale Mother.
We will have to do it. So that,

among the peoples, you may sit like the others,
no longer a mockery, no longer a fear.
But a hope.
Then I shall settle down
in your Barracks. And be content.
Germany, my Mother. My language.

EIGHT POEMS

From *Árvore do Mundo* (*"Tree of the World"*)

CARLOS NEJAR

Translated from the Brazilian Portuguese and introduced by Giovanni Pontiero

CARLOS NEJAR's *Tree of the World*

Giovanni Pontiero

> I am man
> and stone,
> a rigid plain
> and crest of lilies;
> a savannah flower
> laden with sorrows.

("My Science Is the Universe")

At the age of forty, Carlos Nejar already ranks as one of the most influential poets writing in Brazil today. His first book of poems, *Sélesis* (1960), was published in Porto Alegre, and a steady output of verse soon followed. In 1970, when the poet's sixth book of poems, *Ordenações* (*"Ordinations"*), received the prestigious Jorge de Lima Prize, his work began to attract a wider audience, and a progressive perfection of technique has firmly established Nejar's reputation beyond the frontiers of his native Rio Grande do Sul. More recently, translations of his poems in Spanish and German, and now in English, have helped to arouse considerable interest abroad.

The growing volume of essays devoted to Nejar's poetry stresses the immediacy and extraordinary vigor of his writing. Taut structures and bold images convey an overwhelming sense of authority and discipline. To this extent, the parallels drawn between Nejar and other notable Brazilian poets, such as Carlos Drummond de Andrade and João Cabral de Melo Neto, seem altogether relevant. All three poets have succeeded in preserving the intimacy of provincial scenes and traditions in Brazil alongside a universal vision of contemporary man.

So far, most critics have chosen to emphasize the prophetic resonances in Nejar's poetry as he sets about examining the "bones beneath the undergrowth of obscure interrogation" ("Via Sacra"), but his trenchant statements and thought-provoking aphorisms seed almost as many doubts as they do truths. Imponderable mysteries are ultimately more tantalizing for the poet than any firm conclusions.

The title of Nejar's eleventh book of verse, *Árvore do Mundo* ("*Tree of the World*"), from which the following poems have been extracted and translated, is no mere cliché. Besides the obvious symbolism of growth and proliferation, the reader will discover a dense labyrinth of mysterious forms emanating from a solid trunk of organic unity. As a metaphor of existence, Nejar's *Tree of the World* betrays as many gnarled branches and withered buds as miraculous fruits and flowers. To penetrate its foliage is to confront the dark essence of elemental existence. Yet to witness destruction is to discover signs of renewal.

The eternal conflict between human ideals and the frustrating limitations of one imperfect state is examined anew in these poems. The poet unearths "castigated bones / observing the penance / of some ancient psalm" ("Via Sacra"). Elsewhere, he invokes a personal deity. Here the moods fluctuate between anguished yearning, "I seek the face of God" ("On the Wall"), and a chilling fatalism, "God neither begins / nor ends / He is execution ("Rustling Leaves"); between defiant conflict, "for we are ferocious friends and enemies" ("All Is Completed"), and total rejection, "No God presides over me / I am eternal / wavering amidst things / I choose to renege" ("My Science Is the Universe").

Universal problems abound in this book—the blurred frontiers of time and space, the relentless search for meaning and unity in the world around us, man's inevitable solitude and his encroaching decline and transcience: "Ephemeral, we cannot know / how long things may endure" ("The Threaded Needle"). Absurdity and an "incredible violence" taint all human activity: "This mad circus / the splintered wheel of life" ("Life's Roundabout").

A persistent struggle against failure and oblivion constitutes Nejar's life history and everyone's life history. Experience and knowledge consistently reaffirm our gradual impoverishment as human beings: "Ever more poor / we sell at cost price or even less / the sun, the moon, the stars" ("Debt").

Fragments gathered from traditional philosophies and religions underline the contradictory nature of human destiny. Ambivalent forces determine our compromised existence. Man's disordered days are mocked by the twofold concepts of execution (=fulfillment and sentence), freedom (=liberty and responsibility), and pact (=agreement and commitment).

But despite the inequalities of the human struggle against pain and ultimate death, to "Hope, love, create" ("Against Hope") is a mandate. As a spokesman of his age, Nejar has no intention of abdicating this responsibility. Fully conscious of his role as a spiritual "liaison between the soul and the people" ("My Science Is the Universe"), life here and now constitutes the essence and justification of Nejar's poetry. He exposes sorrow, injustice, and despair in order to teach courage and survival. Numerous failures have taught him resilience: "And from so much falling, I rise once more" ("Under a Bullet") and spiritually purged by suffering, the poet finds redemption in love. Nejar defines love as the "highest constellation" ("All Said and Done"), whatever the sacrifices involved: "Things, things / I have loved you to excess. / And you cost me / the universe" ("Things, Things").

The poems in this key collection reveal an experienced hand in matters of technique. Deliberate economy is further enhanced by Nejar's painstaking search for the exact word and phrase. A stark linear quality evokes the infinite horizons of the poet's native pampa even while scanning a transcendental world beyond all frontiers. Isolated verses emulate the perfected concision of the Oriental *haikai,* such as the following description of the universe, "A world shrouded in moss / an undiscovered sky" ("Gregorian Chant"), or where the poet defines the futility of all human effort, "Mankind is an oar / the fatherland a stationary vessel" ("The Shoulder of Things").

The recurring idea of a static world unaffected by human frenzy is captured in striking juxtapositions, in suggestive parallels and reiterations. Vague similes are rejected in favor of incisive metaphors: "Featherless sky / ground / gait / the shoulder of night" ("On the Shoulder of Things"). Every apparent conclusion provokes further questioning in the reader's mind, such as when Nejar affirms that "To exist / is a lapse of patience" ("All Is Completed").

The poems in the closing section of the book, under heading "The Fire of Conscience," provide another important dimension. Composed at greater length and on a quieter note, these poems turn to a deeper analysis of Nejar's inner self. At the same time, he provides valuable insights into his concept of the poet's role. Nejar sees himself as the man who denies in order to affirm, who rebels in order to accept, who strikes out in order to embrace, who dies in order to live. And one final irony reveals "Our life span between two poles / enjoining tides and astrolabes" ("My Science Is the Universe").

The passion and fury that consume Nejar as he probes the inherent paradoxes of the human condition now explode within rather than without, and the poet retreats from the experience physically and emotionally spent: "Like some madman / before the abyss / like some madman / plunging into / the train of the sea / I have exhausted / my entire share of seeing" ("My Science Is the Universe").

São Paulo
August 1979

AGAINST HOPE

We must hope against hope.
Hope, love, create
against hope
only to despair of hope
yet go on hoping
while a trickle of water, an oar,
fishes
exist and survive
amidst conflicts;
while a loom spins
and day breaks forth
like a new garment.

We must hope
for a little wind
and the morning reveille.
No great hope here.
Only a short circuit
in the memory. Hairs,
a swallow's nest and
torrential rains. Hope,
a dog,
chasing across a field
or a tiny hare
that night ill conceals.

The universe is a roof top
with low-set gutters
and the stars, a swarm
of bees around the edges.

We must hope against hope
like the hand fastening
its grip on the lance.

And the essence of hope
is never to arrive;

its face is always something more.
We must despair of
hope
like a bucket in the sea.

One bucket too many
tossed against hope
and over our heads.

THINGS, THINGS

In defiance of love,
all things without exception
were cast out to sea.
I felt no desire to detain them.
I could perceive no return.
Things, things
I have loved you to excess.
And you cost me
the universe.

All my possessions
put up for auction.
The air sold off.
The rivers.
The seasons.

I purchased measures of rain
for my orchard.
I brought moisturing mist
dragging it
past death.
I purchased night
and gave a furtive glance
at the horizon.

Things, things
I have loved you to excess.

SHOES OF FEAR

We awaken trembling
beneath the clocks of fear:
one on our wrist, another in our blood,
yet another in our breathing
their hours
concealed in advance;
with the earth where sturdy
rose bushes of fear are planted.

We breathe and the air is parched
with hammering fists
and soaring gulls.
We wrap up in fear
with sheets so heavy
that they unfold into nights,
throats, vineyards,
horses trotting along crooked lanes.

We dress, putting on
rains and shoes of fear.
Our days are short. The odor
of living ever shorter.
Even famine is shorter.
And sleep.

And no one is forewarned
of dying prematurely.

UNDER A BULLET

I can already see my death begin,
the gathering strands.

Under the weight of a bullet
yet so light
when falling.

I see the lurking hand, in avarice.
Its weapon of eyelids dispersing
the clouded face, an ovule of darkness
on the surface where I fall
and night's vastness.

I go on falling.

The blood where I fall
is a throat
falling.

Under a clean bullet.

Amidst constellations
I go on falling
amidst the forces of production,
enjoined by covenant.
I go on falling.

A solid bullet
that welds me to the world.
I go on falling

A bullet
casting roots
where it burns out.

Birds soaring as
I go on falling.

In the divided homeland.
Under faces and banners
I go on falling;
into the depths of time,

like some leaf or other,

I go on falling,
I go on falling.

And from so much falling, I rise once more.

ON THE WALL

I desire the face of God.
So deeply
engraved
on the wall before me.
Symbol of elevation.

The face of God
in execution.
His terrible presence.
Not as flower.
But as wind of justice.

I cannot define his touch.
I crouch
beside his image.
A frightened child.

I desire the face of God,
freedom.
Even in execution
or executed.

Long are the hands,
long the lance
of the night I combat.
Long is the execution.

Long his face.

SURVIVAL

I
The breath of existing
and I rebel.

Twenty, forty years
of metaphors
unable
to guarantee
life or survival.

I rebel.
My weapons are words
or what
they erect on guard.

Each soul is a metaphor.
The blue and green
garbing themselves
in another firmament
that exceeds itself
and is metaphor.

But to live is not a metaphor,
litter or statue
in the public square.

It is a direct object
that finds itself suffering,
among animals and terrors.

One cannot eat a metaphor.
One cannot taste the morning
like a pomegranate
or the evening
on a table of air.

I rebel

Life,
buried and concealed
deeper
than the mine
of syllables.
Where the world
is larger
than the world itself.

II

Certain things invade me.
Like a ship leaking water.
And then I flounder.

Certain things invade me
suddenly.
With hostile eyes.
Helpless I succumb,
dominated and submissive.

When I examine myself,
things have walked
where I cannot probe.

And my signs are clear
of their perpetuity.

PEOPLE

I

I filled my notebooks
in the expanse of childhood.

I filled my notebooks
with the letters of dawn,
Sundays, forests.

I filled my notebooks
with people
and people
I filled with sea.

II

Where I begin and end,
there are people.

Where the sun radiates its message,
there are people.

Where birds migrate,
there are people.

Where the tractor excavates,
there are people.

And the plantation of night:
freedom.

MULTITUDE

Multitude is my name
and my achievement is
that of being alive.

Multitude is my name.
When I suffer
and sorrows crush me
with their wheels of wind
—I am no longer man—
I am an element
between myself and that which vanishes.

Multitude is my name
and if I come from afar
it is not I who stirs.
Souls understand each other
when they tread
a common path.

The collective soul is the cell
of symbols, and the world
the dark window
where things are lost.

Scholars and fools,
with caution and daring
we live.
And to live is an incredible violence.
For no science is greater
than that of being alive.

CERTAIN WAYS OF SPEAKING
WITH A DEAF WOMAN

DOUG CROWELL

An unusual, perhaps unique, event occurs
  Once upon a time, a Deaf Woman paid for my coffee.

On moving
  Whenever I move from one apartment to another, the first thing
I do is to search for a coffee shop whose morning ambience satis-
fies me. The morning's first cup of coffee is an important one for
me, and I insist on drinking it out.
  After moving into the apartment in which I now live, I spent
eleven days in the search for a coffee shop. I have on previous oc-
casions taken even longer—as long as twenty-two days.
  Once, after moving into a new apartment, I found a satisfactory
coffee shop the very next morning. I enjoyed living in that particu-
lar apartment, and sometimes I regret having left it.

On writing
  I write in coffee shops because I find that I am able to write in
such places. I listen to spoons tinkling, to the sounds of paper pack-
ets of sugar being ripped, to voices indistinct. Occasionally one
voice in particular will stand out above the others; when this hap-
pens I pause to listen to the story that voice might have to tell.
Sometimes the stories are good ones, often they are not.

I enjoy breathing through my nose in coffee shops, because I like the warmth of the air, its smell. I am able to distinguish various odors: stale coffee, burnt grounds, the solution used to clean the formica table tops, the smell of people—on their way to work—who have just showered and washed their hair.

I feel that I derive inspiration from my coffee shops.

The coffee shop

The coffee shop in which I now sit mornings is small, independently owned and well run, with a regular clientele—at least from 7:30 A.M. to 9:00 A.M. or so. The menu for breakfast, which is served only from 6:00 A.M. until 9:00 A.M., is a small one.

Coffee				.25
Tea				.15
Milk	small	.25	large	.40
Orange Juice	small	.40	large	.65
Hard-boiled eggs				.15
Toast—white, rye or raisin				.10
Bagel—w/butter				.30
w/cream cheese				.50
Two eggs, toast, hashed browns				.90
” ” ”		—w/juice		1.15
” ” ”		—w/sausage		1.55
” ” ”		—w/bacon		1.65
” ” ”		—w/ham		2.00
” ” ”		—w/steak		2.30

The lunch and dinner menus are more extensive.

I do not think that this coffee shop makes much money in the mornings. There are a dozen small tables, four booths, ten stools at the counter; the morning regulars occupy one booth, seven small tables, and five of the counter stools. This accounting does not include myself—I change places from day to day, sitting one day in a booth, the next at the counter, the next at a small table. This moving about of mine, though I do not mean it to, to some extent upsets, to a small degree, certain of the regulars. No one has yet spoken to me concerning it, however.

The people are tolerant enough here, so that things run smoothly.

The floor plan of the coffee shop

Donut Kitchen		Storage Rooms		Rest Rooms
Donut Display Case	Coffee etc.	Grill		
Display Case	Cash Regis-ter	Counter		
Door				

The coffee shop strikes me as being comfortable enough.

The regulars of the coffee shop

The regulars of my new coffee shop are—with two exceptions—the same "types" which I have encountered in all the previous coffee shops I have frequented. The exceptions I will describe for you in a moment, but as for the others, every morning in my current coffee shop there sits:

At the counter—

a department store television salesman who lusts after the younger waitress, but who feels her to be beneath his station;

two well-dressed, middle-aged businessmen who converse animatedly on the topic of sports;

a tall, thin man I allegorize Enigma who chain-drinks black coffees.

At the small tables—

two pairs of rather-newly-weds, who are the only regulars to eat a breakfast every morning;

two well-dressed, young businessmen who discuss primarily sports, but who speak occasionally of their sexual lives and problems as well;

a spry-and-eager old man, retired, who provides a certain friendly atmosphere on the mornings it is needed;

a sad young woman.

In the booth—

a young, a middle-aged, and an old (there are three, don't

doubt it) collective City Cowboy who greet me every morning with a falsely friendly, "Hidy, Podnah!"

The exceptions are these:
1) the Deaf Woman—who will be described below;
2) a man, like myself, who writes while drinking his morning cup of coffee—he will often pull the table slightly out from the corner and sit so that he is able to face the room; he is older than me, in his mid-to-late thirties, tall, dark-haired, mustachioed, with very intense eyes; he writes very quickly, and often for relatively long periods of time. On occasion the two of us have, while sitting face-to-face sipping coffee, engaged in unspoken duels of words, each writing fiercely and fast, each trying to outlast the other in the sitting. To date there has emerged no clear-cut victor in any of these duels.

The Deaf Woman speaks

On the morning I first entered my current coffee shop (and I have sometimes wondered how much sub- or unconscious effect the incident might have had upon my decision to choose this as the coffee shop I would frequent), I noticed a rather attractive woman sitting on stool #1. The woman was, I guessed, in her mid-thirties, though dressed in the faded denim and polo shirt style of the fashionable twenty-year-old. The effect of her dress was incongruous but not, as it often is, ludicrous; this woman managed to pull it off. When I entered the coffee shop the woman caught my eye and, because I did not then know where one went to order coffee, I stood behind the empty stool to her left. The waitresses behind the counter noticed me but neither made any move to serve me. I stood quietly for several minutes, learning in those minutes that one ordered coffee at the cash register, and not from behind a counter stool. I continued nonetheless to stand patiently behind the stool, waiting to be served. Finally, as the atmosphere seemed to begin to grow uncomfortable, the woman signaled silently to one of the waitresses and I was brought a cup of coffee. I smiled my thanks to the woman and went to sit in one of the booths, sitting so that I might see the woman whenever I glanced up. And every time I did glance up, she was turned a quarter round on her stool, looking back over her shoulder at me. Every time our eyes met, the woman would smile. I refused to respond in any active manner but merely stared at her for a moment and returned to my writing. At last, when I glanced up from my work, the woman was no longer sitting on her stool; she had quietly left the coffee shop. I stood up, re-filled my coffee cup and settled back into my writing.

An hour later as I was leaving, the waitress informed me that my coffee had been paid for by the woman.

A conversation which occurred at the end of my first week at the coffee shop

"Is this woman deaf?" I asked the waitress.

"She can't hear," said the waitress.

"Is this woman mute?" I asked the waitress.

"She can't talk," said the waitress.

An epic battle in the coffee shop

One recent morning I entered the coffee shop in an exaggerated state of exultation. I had been up all night, had been writing and writing well throughout the night, and had come to the coffee shop for my usual morning coffee, expecting all the while that my "streak" would continue as long as I was writing without significant break. As I approached the coffee shop that morning I saw through the window my fellow writer bent over his corner table, writing furiously. As I entered the coffee shop our eyes met, and each of us immediately realized the state of things. The writer glared at me and returned to the page in front of him; I bought coffee and sat down at table #7. The two of us sat directly facing each other, with two small tables and the space between all that was sepa-rating us. Our eyes met a second time, and in that brief second the "battle" was agreed upon, the epic rules nonverbally acceded to. The writer bent to notebook and donut, I to coffee, pen, and paper. The epic battle commenced.

I lost.

Some questions and answers concerning the Deaf Woman

Q: Did I wish her to seduce me?

A: Yes, but she was mute.

Q: Did I wish to seduce her?

A: Yes, but she was deaf.

Q: Did I sometimes wonder what her history was?

A: Yes. My primary interest in this regard revolved around whether or not her defects were congenital. Had she always been deaf? Had she always been mute? If not, I wondered, how exactly did she feel about no longer being able to speak, no longer being able to hear?

Q: Did the Deaf Woman write?

A: I never saw her write.

Q: Did the Deaf Woman have friends?

A: On only two occasions did I ever see the Deaf Woman in public, outside the coffee shop. Once I saw her in a dress shop, alone, holding dresses up before her body, looking at herself in the mirror. The second time I saw her, the Deaf Woman was sitting on a bench in the park, and a man was sitting beside her. During the brief time I spent looking at them, neither moved.

Q: Did the Deaf Woman live by herself?

A: She lived in a house, not very far from the coffee shop. I never found out whether or not she lived alone.

Q: Did the Deaf Woman buy a dress?

A: I do not know. I only saw her through the dress shop window, for a moment, as I passed.

Q: What was the Deaf Woman wearing in the park?

A: She was not wearing a dress. She had a flower in her hand. Her hair was in a different style.

Q: Have I ever seen the Deaf Woman wearing a dress?

A: No.

Q: Had the Deaf Woman anything to offer me? Any word to speak to me? Any story to tell?

A:

On my interaction with the Deaf Woman

One very fine morning—*the sun shone sharply, the weather was warm, the wispy crisp clouds curved long and languorous*—I re-imagined (wrongly) the pastoral, and found myself feeling mischievous, perhaps even randy. On this fine morning, it was I who paid for the Deaf Woman's coffee. When the Deaf Woman left the coffee shop I followed her, silently, home.

What occurred between the two of us shall be spoken of only by the Deaf Woman.

A poem written, in loose iambic, by the Deaf Woman

How would you solve this domestic crisis?
You've laid down the law about bulbsnatching.
You've warned that when the bulb is swiped from
The study lamp, and the hall light robbed to fill
The reading lamp, somebody's sure to strain
His eyes or sprain her ankle in a darkened
Hallway. And then what happens? Father tries
To snatch a bulb for his workbench—and Junior
Catches him in the despicable act.

What to do? Send Pop to the nearest store
For a fresh supply of new GE bulbs!
Put an end to bulbsnatching forever—
And be sure Pop gets GE bulbs, because
General Electric Lamp Research
Works constantly to make GE Lamps *Stay
Brighter Longer*—and solve these family tiffs pleasantly.

It is my opinion that the concluding alexandrine lends a certain *je ne sais quoi* to the Deaf Woman's poem.

How to do it if every other method fails
    With your hands.

THE CRUCIFIXION

JEAN COCTEAU

Translated from the French by Charles Guenther

1

Most Serene. The hurdles
on the tree. The ladder
on the dead standing tree.
The ladder standing on the dead
tree. The knob
of tears.
Then they saw the barbed
wire. The shadow. Then
they saw the chestnut
of nails. The veins
of the wood. The man's veins.
The intersecting roads. The cloth
that tied the roads
over each other and the motionless wind
and the blinds torn down.
They saw the hurdles tied
and untied. The shadow. The tip of the beams.
The doorleaf. The notch. The bridegroom.
The scarecrow bristling its wings.

The lowly rosebush. The cooper's
ladder.

2

A hurdle. A standing hedge
of thorns. The mire
of sleep. Sunlight
across a shipwreck.
Oysters mussels and other
dead shells on the crushed
tree of shipwrecks.
Who I ask you sticks
to the windows
Who? This white crust
of frost in the shape
of a figure skinned
alive.

3

Most Serene. Instead of a mandrake a root
of entrails springs out
What a shape it has! Like a conflagration
petrified by water.
What water! By the glue
of egg-whites by the bonfire
of madmen by the drop
of the shops' iron curtain.
Made of wax and needles.
Of cries driven with hammer
blows into the nervous
system of a tree
of Judea.

4

Bloody liver spread out on
hedgerows of thorns on a snare
of vicious thorns
of mulberry trees whose mulberries
stain the table with dreadful

spots. Staining the wash
that dries on the barbed
wire. In the sun
the tablecloths dry dragging
in the mud. The sheets
hang inhabited by the grimace of a
shadow play of false
whiteness with real hands.

5
Tell me where the cross
hurts. I'll tend the wound
with cold wide open lips
shouting its cry.
I'll hear the flute of the spine
so light that the skeleton
hangs only by a thread because
of the bag of blood of the bag
of spit of the bag of bile
of the bags hung clumsily on a slim
waist that's cut in two.
Tell me where the cross hurts.
I'll dress it with pads and gauze
and stick a red cross
on top.

6
The square-cut tree hardly
recognizable in that
uncommon form spreads
two branches
equally squared off where
the pulse and arteries
were seen beating so wildly
that the body's tunnels
were filled
with the crush of a mob
chasing a frightened man.

7

The body was bathed abused
boned sullied ravaged
pierced disjointed
raised bent bedded down perched up
bound nailed unnailed
drawn quartered
split cast spilt
hanged stretched pulled down
spread out hoisted decked out
paraded slapped flogged
marked for all eternity
from the twisted signboard
to the boots of the sewer-workers.

8

The infernal machine was driven
by calculations
unknown to the engineers
of a series of ladders
forbidden to the chimney sweepers
under penalty of death. For all
eternity driven to the very
heart of the drama the machine
with disgusting precision
regulated beyond
the candelabrum of the stars.

9

Have you ever seen so many ladders?
Have you ever seen over a lofty
narrow space such
a palisade a cage of rainshowers
so intricate such
an enterprise of scaffolding? Have you ever
seen so many spider
webs around beams?
So many ladders? A true
war machine

against a wall of ramparts.
This aerial disarray
of balconies of sewer grills
of parapets and other grills
of butchers and bakers
of prisoners making signs
to young girls. A scrawl
written in Hebrew but I insist:
of ladders ladders among them
scaling them kicking
elbowing beating
wings of swallows' cries.

10

By the scarlet ladder came
barefoot bearers invisible
firemen of
disgusting indiscretion.
Coming going jostling each other
from below from
above across
the blood clots of the holly the lacework
of hate of the nettles.
And what am I saying? The firm sky
believed by us space all
that on the point of a pin
pricked *somewhere else*
by different and indifferent hands.
It's a matter it's
(between us) a laughing
matter.

11

There were the blows. The blows
of iron on iron. The old rose
of the winds. The blows. The blight
of blows on the bony fan
of the feet. On the matting
of toes. On the boards. On

the exquisite illumination of the missal
of nerves where pain runs
faster than pain
in the coral of torture racks.
The echo of blows. Medallions
of blows. Ears
of blows. Soul of wood. The soul
of blows without a soul.
Blows of the cooper. Blows
of the carpenter. Bowls
of blue meat. Signposts
of the hand's
paths. Neck
of the swan.

12

A job well done. What a strange
promenade. What funeral
ceremonies. What a cap
made of briars. What warmth. What barter
to the loss of a race
skilled in bartering. What a day
of dupes. I ask
permission to speak they deprive me of it.
They bind him. They
flog him. They spit
on him. Those dirty pigs.

On the bridge in this extreme
disorder the pirates victims
of a spell organized
a scanty existence of emigrants at the base
of multicolored unforgetting sleep
which remains from masts
reduced to the use of a gallows
under a storm of shirts.
The toe of a foot in the eye
of the storm tip to tip with
the tips of banners. Illegible

emblems: Bulls'
horns horses' tails goats
eagles in rags.

14
On the too renowned
plot of grass there jostle
the knucklebones of a skeleton
artfully decorated with fly
specks. The soldiers
in clusters of Greco-Roman
wrestling. The equestrian statue
whose horse's snort splashes
foam on the carcass
of a fireworks in the outskirts
where the dead suns
are nailed.

15
The captain of guards
in a bad mood for he
had a rendezvous commands
the units on a strutting horse whose shanks
fall into the very ground.
Flicking its tail it chases
green flies which really
don't know which
way to turn.
Ceremonial analogy to the spectacle
of slaughters hung with raw meat
with gold leaves with knotted
ribbons.

16
Gordian. Such was the knot
of muscles of ropes
of one of the vultures thinking of nothing
but mischief or fighting
at the end of a kind

of greasy pole. He lives
badly he foresaw
a ladder with beatings
climbed by a white
horde of cooks plucking geese.
Then a cock blew the trumpet.
The high became low: *Plunge!*
Plunge! they shouted to him
from the kitchens.

17

An accident happened
so fast. The other
scarecrow too heedful
of its transformation into branches
of a tree into knots of a tree into bones
of a tree a whole bark
of a skin of a gnarled pine which bleeds
and cracks enclosed in an almost mythological
dream frightened the angels crying: *Hurry, hurry!*
There isn't a minute
to lose. Those simple things
circling around
crying their lungs out and losing feathers
which blinded him and stuck
to his wounds.

18

Most Serene. The shield
of murders.
Kneeling
animals weep. The keys to number
seven. The triangular
wheel of miracles.
The hand
which isn't one of them. The eye
which isn't one of them.
The mortal sickness
of dream. The simple

difficulty of being. The sleeping
Bohemian girl. The castle
of the game of chess. Its free
bishop.

19
On a black school desk
where she raises
her June-bugs death
bites her nails bites her penholder
licks the golden beetle of the purple
ink bites a ruler and licorice
erases and draws lines
bites the mottled blotter
draws more lines sticks out her tongue
squints licks the beetle
under the (how impudent!) eyes of the priest
But why doesn't he notice
that she
copies.

20
The whole stupefied organism ejects
its liquid
to escape the muddy roads
which have become impassable.
It begins
under the arms makes detours
gets lost regroups and forms a fluvial
network of anatomy.
The disaster came from rusty nails crushing
the very fragile machinery of a factory
accustomed to working at night without lights.
That's why the whole inside
ran out
looking for an escape.
That agonizing water caught on the corner
of the scarcely living cornices
its drops mad with fear leaping
desperately into the void.

21

What can't be said (and yet
what can't I say with
my way of compelling words
to be silent) what can't
be said is the honey
of the bees of agony. It
flows from their hive it binds
with a dizzying infected gauze
lost profiles at the base
of a caduceus. One can guess
what it's made of.

22

And now a profile
of a turned-up face joined to the vinestock
of legs by
a cloth of a blue like the red
holds
a pillar of salt balanced
on its forehead. And that other face
with a profile misshapen because
of its knob of tears
sticks its cheek against the dreadful
resin.

23

A thunder of beribboned vehicles with seats
a thunder of clusters of acacia and
a thunder of marriage beds
dragged upstairs
a thunder of barricades
a thunder of cannon
a thunder of men shouting: *Over there!*
Over there! A thunder
of lands decked out with flags applauds
to heaven a spurt
of blood turned into wine. Angel Cégeste
blew the trumpet. And the shadow

of the object standing up again became
the object.

24
It tore the cloth of silence
from east to west. Silence
was heard crying in such
a way that it was intolerable
to the heart's ears. A
spray of ink for certain
full of masterpieces
spattering a black flight
of compromising papers burned in haste.
While a torrential rain
of bayonets
finished off the victims savagely.

25
Kneeling right
and left. Alone alas
of my species (no matter
to be proud of) under a coat
of mail made of figures under
a clamorous armor
kneeling alone left
and right—the snow with a blind woman's hands
spreading a tablecloth—I close
kneeling alone of my species
alas in this room where the crime
occurred the yellow
mouth of my learned
wound able
to utter a few words.

TWO POEMS

From *Manuscritos*

NICANOR PARRA

Translated from the Spanish by Steven White

ANY WOMAN X

A prostitute that came to be the richest woman in the world
Had a cathedral built, a kind of model city
Equipped with barbershops, soda fountains, amusement parks
Equipped if I'm not mistaken with tombs, equipped with trees
In whose branches you could see birds, you could see nests
Filled with eggs that the whore gathered
for her breakfast.

In the interior of that cathedral she erected her whorehouse
That was open Friday and Saturday from eleven to twelve
On the basis of fireworks, on the basis of eunuchs
Whose work consisted in taking care of the clients
Offering them chairs and offering them a little boiled water.

The intelligent prostitute didn't comply with this;
She had a tabernacle built inside the whorehouse

Where she had the bones and clothes of the saints deposited
The names of the national heroes engraved in bronze
She had all kinds of objects deposited there.
The following maxims she had engraved at the entrance to her
    bedroom.

Five minutes is the minimum, fifteen minutes is the maximum.
Humanity can wait for a few minutes.
The lay bums can come in first, then their sons,
Then everyone else can come in, if there's time for them.
Eternity can also make us ephemeral
If we look through a telescope filled with condensed milk.

To defend this fortress she had a revolver built
In whose handle she had the following maxim engraved:
"The road of excess leads to the palace of wisdom"
I talked to this prostitute point blank
While she was getting naked in front of a mirror.
I asked her why she had spent her money so foolishly
She told me that her family had died years ago
And that she was a monomaniac for sex.

Well, all right, I answered while eating a sandwich
In no time at all remarkable things will happen.
She wasn't wrong in that a kind of dog
Or perhaps a cat my memory is failing me
Made its appearance from a little tunnel
That was going from one tabernacle to another
From a reliquary it passed imperceptibly to a typewriter
And leaning its paws against a bidet said:

Perhaps you find my presence a little strange
In reality I don't have any teeth at my disposal
My head of hair is a simple crust of bread.
For the following act it barked awhile
And from its mouth came a piece of emerald
Accompanied by a small column of smoke.
After that it disappeared leaving behind on a written paper:

"I am the planter of these lands"

Years later I returned to visit that place,
My prostitute friend received me underground
There she was reading the Bible, reading the *luisíadas*
Bound in a yellow web
She took off her clothes and we began our excavations.

MISSION ACCOMPLISHED

planted trees	17
sons	6
published works	7
total	30
surgical operations	1
fatal falls	17
cavities	17
total	35
tears	0
drops of blood	0
total	0
current kisses	48
tongue "	17
in front of the mirror "	1
luxurious "	4
Metro-Goldwyn-Mayer "	3
total	548
socks	7
underwear	1
towels	0
sport shirts	1
handkerchiefs	43
total	473

world maps	1
bronze candelabra	2
gothic cathedrals	0
total	3

humiliations	7
waiting rooms	433
barbershops	48
total	1534901

european capitals	548
lice and fleas	333333333
Apollo 16	1
total	49

glandular secretions	4
best men for the wedding	7
nuts and bolts	4
total	15

literary jewels	1
fathers of the Church	1
aerostatic balloons	17
total	149

CEZANNE

SIDNEY GOLDFARB

    a. they do not seem at a loss for words
    b. the party of verbal conspirators
    c. a young girl brushing her hair
    d. there is some impulse to go on
    e. from what to be saved: the sickness
    f. from what to be led: the bitterness
    g. the man who hurts me
    h. the woman who hurts me
    i. they go out in a nest of stars
    j. dog pushing head thru rickety door
    k. man dancing in blanket
                  l. peligro
         m. holding his crotch
n. mamacita
        m. holding his crotch
            o. earning an honest buck
                    p. broke
p. it would appear to be broken
p. roto, descompuesto
        q. and they are circling
r. oiseau tranquil que nidifie en l'air oiseau
      b. verbal conspirator
          r. oiseau

r. oiseau
  a. a sound
r. double voice of bluejay
    s. willing to dance
r. mountain chickadee
    a. no loss for words
c. a young girl quietly brushing her hair
   l. le danger, peligro
e&f. butterness-sickness
    i. nest of stars
s. willing to dance
s. if there is ever
 a chance to love
 I will love you now
 here at this airport
    a. no loss for words
   b. verbs
    c. my daughter quietly
     brushing her hair
d. the impulse
   e. the saving grace
     f. bitterness dying
      in a nest of stars
g. man who speaks cruelly
    j. dog pushing in
   m. holding his crotch
n. mamacita! (exclamation)
     o. we need money
h. the woman who hurts me
    s. willing to dance
 t. my name
   s. if there is ever a chance to love
   I will love you now
   here in this airport
   (where my car
   is a little too dirty)
h. (has she found
 someone smoother?)
   l. peligro

m. holding his crotch r. oiseau

                            r. birds passing over
                                poems in their beaks

h. have you found
   someone smoother?

                       c. the young girl smoothing her hair
                       r. qui nidifie en l'air

 t. my name

              a. my name

                   m. my name

u. your name

              u. are not leaving this airport
                there are planes to Paris

a. manamana
   fish-like-earth

                     o. lonely money thief
                       paracataca
                     p. completamente decompuesto

d. this impulse to you
   (I will love you
     at this airport)

                  d. impulso
                  willing to dance

q. and they are circling
   they are holding their pattern

                          v. they are waiting for us

 t. my name

              v. voice of bluejay
              broken in two

w. double voice

          x. are you ready?

y. y . . . . y . . . . y . . . .
  you . . . y . . . y . . . .
  yes . . . . . we can . . .
  . . . . oh yes we can

                   z. oiseau tranquil
                   Cezanne
                   and I will love you now
                   here in this airport

where the planes leave for Paris
and the broken old cars
set down the road for New Mexico
Thursday
Thursday
Thursday
Cezanne
oiseau
zed

Rannit

The violin
of Monsieur
Ingres

& Estonian
lines written
in English

Give me the artificial flowers,
the glories of metal and glass.

Kavafis

Glass flowers —
let them try to beget.

Viereck

Metal flowers

Dark silver

Dark silver, thorium, pewter,
slow turning, hope deferred,
it stands
above beauty
your
handmade word.

In looking

In looking
one aims
to retell

The seas
mountains
clouds,

but to see
is to forget
the names
of things.

*L*ight, what is

Light, what is the light of blood,
the real unfaithful light?
What is your true mysterious second anima?
Birch-feminine and willow-shy —
        you are in life;
in art — magnificent male animal.

The impulse

The impulse of light
can never be flame,
never broken the movement of column,
surrender yourself
to thunder of flames
and conquer
        the body of color.

To. your cut

To your cut and hammered rhyme,
your Doric splendor,
divided light   flaring across,
rhyme — fragile firm embrace,
breath on breath,   breathing.

Rhyme — the two defined hands
of your stanza, rhyme straithening
at the cliffedge of line,

rhyme — marshy Lethe's delta
and clear black Pierian crystal
shimmering in its phrase,
rhyme — frieze, portico, architrave
and the star-blue syllable.

Rhyme —
            two horses of Platonic soul
watching.

Your line

Your line is like an angel's
wing. Then line fruit
celestial, clean. Your roots
are in the earth of light.

My threefold angel

My threefold angel —
forgiveness,
friendship,
verse.
No frienzied earth
or anger.
Only the gray amber
of your eyes
and the gray skies
in the highest trees
of our small graveyard.

Only the syllable's breeze.

Flute

Flute, not trombone,
not Bachus's son,
your syllable's bone
washed by the sun.

I saw you

⎯⎯⎯⎯⎯⎯⎯⎯⎯⎯

I saw you in my dream,
you had the same pure gray
tender touch, but
the names of your children
were different and
you had a new
four month old daughter
called Naomi.

There was no name for our happiness,
our beds were placed together
in the house of farthest
terminal patients.
The terrible is
only the beginning
of beauty.

On Her
Dancing Ravel's
"Pavan for a
Dead Infanta"

1.

I would like
to be one
to be one
who has read
the ardor
of all your partings.
The Infanta is dead
but you are the fate and light
of Delos.

2.

An Elegiac Disfich

Dancer or swallow?
to dream of that
flowing perfection?
Bride of Apollo
you turn
Grecian,
Patricia McBride.

She has returned

She has returned, her
cliff-face veiled in that
famous fume of the
master. Grown beyond
herself she has changed
no more, faithfully
wearing no jewels.
For nearly two full days
I watched her in an
upper gallery of the
museum. Mute and high
she stood in a kind of
earthen honor, her divine
fruitless hands anchored
in themselves. Yes, I
saw her with my own
strange hands:

                              she was
standing there below her
portrait, standing under
it, not knowing
why
        she smiled.

    When was it that
I saw her for the first time?
— Years ago,
when she was
a little child.
I remember well
her delicate neck —
she was kneeling in our
church of Santa Maria
Novella... Somebody told me
that her name was
Lisa Gherdini.

My bird

My bird,
my brittle birch,
sing.
Lines are silent,
sadness is ceasing
and somewhere
the Poor Man of Assisi
is crying
/my/ Brother Fire.

My bird,
my second
birth.

The trees

The trees — now bare,
unvoiced, unfleshed,
raise swaying snow-drafts
and hang them on the sky.

Nor leaf, nor bird,
your word
stripped to ribbed time.

Apostrophize this destitute
sweet purity.

Of the segments of this cycle the following ones are written for —

"Dark Silver" — for Pauline Hanson, "In looking" — for Daniel Brush, "The Trees" — for James Laughlin, "The Impulse" — for Joan Thorne, "To your cut" — for H. D., "Your line" — for Naum Gabo, "Flute" — for James L. Weil, "On her dancing" — for Patricia McBride, "Light, was it" — for Emily Dickinson. / Lisa Gherardini is the maiden name of Mona Lisa Gioconda.

SELECTED POEMS OF
PATIENCE WORTH

Edited by Stephen E. Braude

The poems which follow demand a brief explanation, since they were produced through a Ouija board and through automatic writing in the early part of this century. From 1913 to the mid-1930s a personality calling herself Patience Worth manifested itself through the medium of Pearl Curran, a St. Louis housewife. Mrs. Curran had only an eighth-grade education, modest musical ability, and no apparent literary ability (judging in part by her own attempts to produce poetry and fiction, once the communications had begun). Yet Patience Worth, the personality, produced several novels and thousands of poems, many of which were hailed at the time as works of high quality and perhaps even genius. Patience claimed to be the surviving spirit of a woman who lived in England in the eighteenth century, and communicated in a variety of styles, ranging from fairly modern to arcane and archaic. The personality revealed in the communications, however, was consistent throughout with respect to such things as moral outlook, sense of humor, pet phrases, and favorite images.

The Patience Worth communications caused quite a stir for a while, and provoked intense research into the possible explanations for Patience Worth's (or Pearl Curran's) literary output. The investigators, however, were unable to explain this case in any satisfying way, and eventually the public lost interest in Patience Worth, both as a psychological or possible psychic phenomenon and as a source of valuable literature. Apart from a recent book recounting the entire story of Patience Worth (I. Litvag, Singer in the Shadows, New York, Macmillan, 1972), the following selection of poems is the first time in more than forty-five years that any sizable selection of the poetry has found its way into print. Whatever one

*may think about the case as a whole, the Patience Worth material is un-
doubtedly the finest literary work to have been produced mediumistically.*

*Since most of Patience Worth's poetry was produced via a Ouija board,
the poems were delivered without indications of such things as capitali-
zation, punctuation, or parsing into lines and stanzas. All the published
versions of the poetry therefore represent a joint creative venture, involv-
ing the source (whatever or whoever it was) of the words and the editor
who parses and punctuates them. I have experimented with numerous dif-
ferent parsings of the following poems, each of which seems to me to
have its own merit. Since I doubt whether there are any clear guidelines
to follow in a case such as this (after all, the works, whatever their style,
were produced in this century), I encourage the reader to try reparsing
the poems. I do not pretend that the versions which follow are the only
acceptable ones, much less the best. Although in the absence of any
clear guidelines this might seem to be an awesome task, perhaps subse-
quent editors of Patience Worth's poetry can take some comfort from the
following lines from Patience.*

> *I am molten silver, running.*
> *Let man catch me within his cup.*
> *Let him proceed upon his labor,*
> *Smithing upon me.*
> *Let him with cunning smite my substance.*
> *Let him at his dream,*
> *Lending my stuff unto its creation.*
> *It shall be no less me.*

—S.E.B.

THE SOUNDS UNHEARD BY MAN

I have heard the moon's beams sweeping the waters,
Making a sound like threads of silver, wept upon.
I have heard the scratch of the pulsing stars,
And the purring sound of the slow moon as she rolled across
     the night.
I have heard the shadows slapping the waters,
And the licking sound of the wave's edge as it sinks into
     the sand upon the shore

I have heard the sunlight as it pierced the gloom with a golden bar

Which whirred in a voice of myriad colors.
I have heard the sound which lay between the atoms which danced
  in the golden bar.
I have heard the sound of the leaves reclining upon their cushions
  of air,
And the swish of the willow-tassels as the wind whistled upon them,
And the sharp sound which the crawling mites proclaim upon the
  grasses' blades,
And the multitudes of sounds which lie at the root of things.
Oh, I have heard the song of resurrection which each seed makes
  as it spurts.
I have heard the sound of the night's first shadow when it
  intermingles with the day,
And the rushing sound of Morning's wings as she flies o'er the
  Eastern gateway.

All of these have I heard.
Yet man hath not an ear for them.
Behold, the miracle He hath writ within me,
Letting the chord of Imagination strum!

THE SOUNDS OF MEN

I have heard the music men make,
Which is discord proclaimed through egotry.
I have heard the churning of water by man's cunning,
And the shrieking of throttles which man addeth unto the day's
  symphony.
I have heard the pound of implements and the clatter of blades.
I have heard the crushing blasts of destruction.
I have heard old men laugh,
And their laughs were rusted as old vessels in which brine
  were kept.
I have heard women chatter like crows o'er carrion
And laugh as a magpie o'er a worm.

I have beheld all of these and heard them.
Men have ears for such.
And the mystery of man is that he should present them and cry,
"Sing! Sing, poet! Sing!"

SHADOWS

Shadows!
Little winging shadows, flitting like grey birds beneath the
    leaf bower.
Sombre shadows, beclouding shadows, swept forward, blotting out
    the sun.
Shadows, thin silver shadows, little fleck-clouds passing o'er
    the moon's face.
Shadows, crimson shadows, the touch of the scarlet sun lingering
    upon the eve's sombre robes.
Shadows, purple shadows, lined delicately against the night by
    the silver of the moon,
Like shining dust upon its royal garb.
Shadows . . . shadows . . . shadows.
Phantoms? Yet I behold them.

THE NOTE OF BRASS

In that first pale hour
Still blushing from the night's embrace,
When the moon dips o'er the earth's rim
And the sun comes slowly forth;
When the lark opeth its throat
And singing, climbs the still starry sky;
And the brook slips through the dew-wet field,
Whispering cool words, little calm troths;
And the reeds bend low in the marsh;

And the trees are heavy-swaying;
And the sweet scent of the damp grain floats from the valley;
At this holy instant I have oft heard
An ass bray.

CHILD'S PRAYER

I, Thy child forever, play
About Thy knees this close of day;
Within Thy arms I now shall creep,
And learn Thy wisdom while I sleep.
Amen.

WHO SAID THAT LOVE WAS FIRE?

Who said that love was fire?
I know that love is ash.
It is the thing which remains
When the fire is spent,
The holy essence of experience.

PATIENCE WORTH

A phantom? Weel enough,
Prove thyself to me!
I say, behold, here I be,
Buskins, kirtle, cap and pettyskirts,
And much tongue!
Weel, what hast thou to prove thee?

MY SONG

What a rich song would I unloose
Like a flock of restless birds ascending,
Neither clinging to a path,
But swerving out and far and up and down,
Making music knock the dull doors of gloom
To unloose sorrow and let it free.
Oh, I would see it try its heavy wings and forget its weariness,
And speed away to bathe in the sunlight.
I would let forth my melody like a shimmering cloth,
Spun of gold and sapphires.
It shall glint and gleam,
Marking the dull hours with its splendor.
I shall lay it as a footcloth for His sons and daughters.
Lo, I would garland the air with such perfume
That the earth would be bathed of it,
Until the sweetness and the melody should unloose laughter from
    its prison,
Letting it sport with nimble feet
Like some slender fawn poised upon the brink,
Or gracefully skimming o'er the way
And opening up joy to all who would behold it.
Lo, I would work magic and witchery upon my song,
So that no man might not hark.
Lo, I would create a sprite,
Not one whit more than a sandsgrain in height,
And not one whit heavier than down,
So that it might sit within a man's ear
And woo him.
And when he would pluck it forth—
Lo, it would sink deeper, aye,
And lodge within his heart.
He may not deny it, this song.
Oh, I would take the earth by the hand,
And with nimble toes would I spring o'er the rough places,
Taking it after me.
Lo, I would pipe such a lay,
That when Earth had danced until weary,
She would lie down in thankful rest.

I WONDER IF ALL THE TEARS UNSHED

Oh, I wonder if all the tears unshed and shed
Assemble not at the hem of Spring,
Becoming the gentle rains of sweet fruition.
I wonder if all the sighs which trembling come or die bestifled,
Assemble not in some holy spot,
Returning as winds which lash and beat in agony
Or languorously caress.
I wonder, oh I wonder if hope cut down,
The dewy, dewy hope of all the earth.
That sweet sustaining essence which besparkles new each morn,
Becomes not the winter snow,
The white pure ash which sifts upon the dead, dead boughs,
Bedecking them.

WHEN TIME HATH TROD WITH ME

When Time hath trod with me a long, long way,
And we have grown aweary, Time of me, and I of Time,
Will then the mornings seem one half so sweet,
Or the bluebells' coming cease to chime to me?
Or shall I be weary o' the passing things,
No longer see in weary eyes the dying smile,
Or in youth-lit ones the dawn of love?
O will the day be then but a mute trudging on
With Time, who is weary of me,
And I so weary of Time?

THE DECEIVER

I know you, you shamster.
I saw you smirking, grinning,

Nodding through the day,
And I knew you lied.
With mincing steps you gaited before men,
Shouting of your valor.
Yet you, you idiot,
I knew you were lying.
And your hands shook
And your knees were shaking.

I know you, you shamster.
I heard you honeying your words,
Licking your lips and smacking o'er them,
Twiddling your thumbs in ecstasy
Over your latest wit.

I know you, you shamster.
You are the me the world knows.

WHIFF, SAYETH THE WIND

Whiff, sayeth the wind,
And whiffing on its way, doth blow a merry tale.
Where, in the fields all furrowed and rough with corn,
Late harvested, close-nestled to a fibrous root,
And warmed by the sun that hid from night thereneath,
A wee, small, furry nest of root mice lay.
Whiff, sayeth the wind.

Whiff, sayeth the wind.
I found this morrow, on a slender stem,
A glory of the morn, who sheltered in her wine-red throat
A tiny spinning worm that wove the livelong day—
Long after the glory had put her flag to mast—
And spun the thread I followed to the dell,
Where, in a gnarled old oak, I found a grub,
Who waited for the spinner's strand

To draw him to the light.
      Whiff, sayeth the wind.

      Whiff, sayeth the wind.
I blew a beggar's rags,
And loving was the flapping of the cloth.
And singing on I went to blow a king's mantle 'bout his limbs,
And cut me on the crushed gilt.
And tainted did I stain the rose until she turned a snuffy brown,
And rested her poor head upon the rail along the path.
      Whiff, sayeth the wind.

      Whiff, sayeth the wind.
I blow me 'long the coast,
And steal from out the waves their roar.
And yet from out the riffles do I steal the rustle of the leaves,
Who borrow of the riffle's song from me at summertide.
And then I pipe unto the sands,
Who dance and creep before me in the path.
I blow the dead and lifeless earth to dancing, tingling life,
And slap thee to awake at morn.
      Whiff, sayeth the wind.

MY MORNING

Is morning less lovely because rain fell?
Or because the winds were ruthless
And played at havocking about the blossoms?
Is morning less lovely because my eyes are brimming
And my heart is such a little heavy thing,
Beating my bosom with a rhythmic pulse and hurting?

Yet is morning less lovely?
Nay, for her head, even though rain has descended,
Is lifted and interwoven with rainbows,
And the havocking wind has spread a footcloth of leaves,

Some of them perfumed things with honey upon their lips,
Pink and glowing, yea, or crimson bruised.

Oh, what a happy thing that I with brimming eyes
May see this morning.

PATIENT GOD

Ah, God I have drunk unto the dregs,
And flung the cup at Thee!
The dust of crumbled righteousness
Hath dried and soaked unto itself
E'en the drop I spilled to Bacchus,
Whilst Thou, all-patient,
Sendest purple vintage for a later harvest.

HERE IS MY CUP

Here is my cup—
Frail, white-lipped, and I—
O, I would sup,
But the dream is old.
I know dreams;
I have fed upon them,
And there is no substance in the feeding.
I would sup.
There is wine but when I have supped—
There is nothing but more dreams;
Phantasies, phantoms, writhing mysteries,
Bits of chaos which I cannot mould.
I am oppressed with dreaming,
Weary of fancy.
I am hungered for reality.

I am famished as a she-wolf
With a brood to suckle.
For I would feed—aye,
I would feed the brats of fancy—
And there is nothing but dream,
Mocking dream.
God, what a sup!
Green as jade,
Poisonous as the venom of an asp.
Great God, give me reality!

A TWAIN

Lo, a fool in a garden into a window gazed,
Where a monk in solitude prayed and told the hours and beads.
    "Folly, folly!" said the fool,
    And skipped a measure.

Lo, a monk in his seclusion looked forth from his casement
Upon a fool who played with grass tassels or a dragonfly and
        laughed.
    "Folly, folly!" the monk chanted,
    And murmured, "Ave, ave."

FATHER, IS THIS THY WILL?

Father, is this Thy will?
God, the din!
Blood, thick-crusted, still living, I saw it fall unto the dust.
Hunger, gnawing like a wolf whose teeth do whet upon my vitals,
        crouching before me—
A hideous thing, whose hands show dripping, and whose tongue
        doth feed upon the new-sprung streams, licking life from
        living things!

Father, is this Thy will?
Damn the discord garrulously belched forth from burning throats!
Hell is within the eyes that look across the wastes!
Hell crawls upon the earth, dragging her robe of fire—
Sprinkled of scarlet, its hem,
And the sound it makes upon its trailing way is like the shriek of
    womankind in labor!

THE SCORE SHEET

BRETT MASSEAUX

January 13 (Late evening)

SHE closed the drawer to the end table by her bed and neatly dropped the wood chips into the wastebasket. She looked at her thighs. No bruises. Unusual.

Winter had its advantages over summer, at least it did when the snow covered everything. Scratches and scrapes she could deal with, but not the kind caused by sticks and rocks. Besides, there was no one to put liniment on her back.

January 14 (Early morning)

SHE sipped her coffee and mulled over the morning paper. All bad news, it seemed. A man had been killed, repeatedly stabbed about the face and chest. It was the fourth such killing in four weeks, and all had taken place in a large park mere blocks from her apartment.

"*Women* used to have to watch out for themselves," she thought. "Now men do."

January 20 (Early evening—one week later)

SHE hadn't had a walk in the park for a week, and it seemed a good time for one. It had snowed the entire day, and the park looked as if someone had run wild with an enormous can of white paint. The beauty of the scene was marred only by the many foot trails packing the snow along the paths.

"So much the better," she thought. "At least it won't be *my* feet that spoil the smoothness of the snow."

(Late evening)

SHE strolled through the park, breathing in the crisp air.

HE was following her.

SHE stopped, picked up a handful of snow, patted it into a ball, and threw it at a nearby rock. It missed. Undaunted, she tried again. Finally, after three more tries, she succeeded. She gave a shout of triumph.

HE gazed at her from behind a nearby tree.

SHE was enjoying her game, and her aim was improving. She knew there was someone among the trees, but that didn't interrupt her play.

HE looked at her thighs, exposed below her coat. His breathing was deep and fast as he rubbed and scratched at his crotch. He wanted her, and there was no one around to prevent him from having her. Tonight would be good.

SHE turned to the sound of his breathing. It was time.

HE lunged from the brush, and stood, crouched and sinister. It was this first reaction he craved. The first scream, the first indication of terror. But . . . she spoiled it for him. She turned to run before he could see the fear on her face. He started after her. It would be easy. The snow was deep, and she was having trouble keeping her balance.

SHE knew how close he was. She knew he would soon overtake her. The snow was slowing her steps. Suddenly, she felt his hands grab her ankle. Clutching her pocketbook, she tried to break her fall. She heard him laughing, felt him grabbing at her. She beat at his face and tried to kick him. He seemed to enjoy every moment.

HE smiled as he ripped her clothes. Her weak punches made the conquest that much more pleasurable. She was so helpless and pretty. He grabbed a handful of snow, ground it in her face, and penetrated her while she couldn't see.

SHE pushed him, pleaded with him and yanked at his clothes, but he would not stop. She watched him climax, throwing his head back and emitting a loud, raspy cry from his throat. Then he collapsed on her.

HE rolled off, lay back and sighed, contentedly. It *had* been a good night. She had fought. He liked that. And now she was sitting up, holding her head. He could almost predict her next moves. She would reach into her bag for a tissue and dab at her face. Then, she would try to reason with him to let her go, which he would, after he'd raped her again, and threatened to find her if she told anyone. It was all routine—old hat.

HE chuckled as he watched her reach into her pocketbook. He'd been right. She was searching for a tissue. Then his smile faded as she withdrew a large butcher knife, and brought it down, time after time, on his face.

(Late, late evening)

SHE sat on the edge of her bed and opened the drawer to her end table to reveal four neat little notches on the side. With her now clean butcher knife, she carved a fifth notch in the row and carefully dropped the wood chips into the wastebasket.

SHE looked at her thighs. Several bruises were beginning to appear. It had been a good night. He had fought. She liked that. She wouldn't need to walk in the park again for at least a week.

THIRD WAY

ANNALISA CIMA

Translated from the Italian by Sizzo de Rachewiltz, revised by Mary de Rachewiltz

1 BEYOND THE OBJECT

Beyond the object
involution of commonplace-cankered
myths, step up
to inferred convictions.
Vague baffling taking
from functions of sovereign life,
rogatory starry-eye in color.
Diasporas of dissent
have failed to reawaken,
overwhelmed by the sudden
fulmination of a ban
biting and useless.
We want to think, and they too,
your sign of uncertainties
bedlam won wealth
leaves you with the illusion of seeming,
strong with the most recent past.

We want to think, and they too,
free from ataraxy, senses
uprooted rather than rebellious.
Play the card of involution.
The taste of barren unions
achieves not strength of vice:
it will damn your years to the last
and your almighty dollar to extinction.
Nobody will seek to understand you: you shall pass
useless hermaphrodites,
humiliated by thoughtless admiration
corrupters sans corruption.

2 WE WANT TO LIVE

Forbid ourselves judgment, possible
object for the soul, choose
constant values, following
hands written in charcoal,
racial desires hates
successions. One or more without
religions' absorptions, clear
in resolution; once wars
are over, no segregation of colors
of money, no jealousies, the replaced
heart beats, thought vomits beyond,
green turns to blood:
alone at the end not understanding
distant ones are cried, close ones
killed. Just death to stop thinking.
Destinies of ending together
or later but always and all.
We want to live for and how, maybe to
be, not you, you can not:
you want to kill us.
They force us, cast behind the walls

your and my enemies, to think:
he's different, we are
because we want to, only
and without, it does not matter how, but
live and kill us ourselves,
to resolve unto Him if we believe
if it is worth if it is. Without executioners:
hearts of black flesh and paper
hair, with or without money.
We don't want people with multicolored
tails, everybody has his
own death, I want to know mine, not
tell it. Think of your brother, stop
the machine that is crushing him, cure
the cancer that eats him, devour your money
and don't tell, don't kill to
sanctify them, not all blood is
sacrifice, not all blood
generations, kill to believe in the
meaning of things. We,
and they too, want to live.

3 PASSIVE SENSIBILITY

Your degree, mine
of translatism,
organic disorganic,
or practical reason.
Pathicus, lascivious:
if the sensitive is so
why evade, have you
the dynamics to do it?
Every reduction to the
sensitive abolished: if yes
seek further. Quench
the thirst for shrink. Shout

your degree, mine
of translatism:
have no fear.

4 HARMONY

Order of the world as was
the Pythagorean,
communication between monads.
Given a and b the subsequent
of a is equal to the subsequent of b
the two terms are the same.
Harmony number cohesion
perfect watches
with odd numbers, unable
to understand
undistinguished distinctions.
Object and cause do not
mingle in the unity of
the foundation, depth,
not struggle, but harmony achieved.

5 BEWUSSTSEIN

Having recognized
an inner reality, the sage has
conscience: virtue becomes
commonplace and conscience
fades.
Mistaken about his life,
so far from
lost habits, only for a
sphere of inwardness, which is:

reality overhead. Need to go back
over ourselves and become
what we want to
see.

6 ABDERITISM

Not progress but static
standstill. Ever questioned
never heard we
live again. The same,
with some problems: yesterday
tomorrow, we made them act.
Authority destiny history:
animal reproduction of facts
sole renewal? In
repetition, fiction of time
is the artificer and the artifice.
Abderitism: conception
of always never-ending.

7 NO TO INDIVIDUALISM

Selfishness in order not to pretend,
to admit besides my own
the existence of
others? Values
for their own sake or just
for those they involve?
Continuous feeling
through disgregation,
not for an
individual I.

8 ART

Principle or metaphysical appearance
one attempted to take from the object
which too was divided in partitions
we want to find in techniques.
Perceptive technique: art
without distinction between higher or
less high, raving inspiration:
We do not want to fall in aesthetics
without catharsis, purged
of phony metaphysics, more real:
in immanence a credo,
in self-destruction find ourselves.

9 FORM

Form has no imperfections
is neither participation nor part:
it fulfills itself. The form you observe
knows us, sets itself against
disgregation: already expected
before the end.

10 CONVERSATION

The hours conversing with yourself:
thought and action, do not
lose them
we have worn out the wall
beyond which we can
find ourselves again,
more real, less realized.

11 THIRD WAY

The third way to
distinguish A con-
sists of the relation between
A and oneself. A
identifies itself, there is
no alternative, hence
monotheism.

12 HAVING DEFIED THE SYSTEM

Having defied the system,
let us throw flowers deny the past,
mating of brothers allowed:
praise to the changing taste,
blessed be the wedlocks of homosexuals:
play waiting for useless yuletides.
Only he who tells man from man
may take part of reality,
witnesses and victims
of previous incarnations.
The system is violence
in the face of ideas.

Vanity that forces to the part
to be represented. A similar
choice comes from habits.
The impotence of nerves, of phalli
is protest against boredom
into which the real hurls us.
Lobby of forgotten merits,
set up against anguish,
to come in order to become, so
coition can find expression:
subtle violence made of flowers
and of let them be.

FINDING MY WAY

WOLFGANG HILDESHEIMER

Translated from the German by Allan Blunden

One evening, about a year ago, I had a visit from my uncle. He brought me two pictures as a present, and told me he had acquired them for a very reasonable figure at an auction. They were genuine oil paintings, large and heavy, done on canvas in an elaborate impasto style and mounted in massive gilt frames. They both depicted alpine landscapes with snow-covered mountains, humble chalets, and woodcutters wending their way toward home. The only significant difference was¹ that one of the landscapes was bathed in the glow of the setting sun, while the other lay beneath the shadow of a gathering storm. As soon as I saw them I knew they had to be called *Alpenglow* and *Before the Storm.*

My uncle proposed that I should hang the pictures there and then. I couldn't think of an excuse not to, so I duly hung them on the wall while he stood and watched. "Oh by the way," he remarked, "they're called *Alpenglow* and *Before the Storm*" "Ah yes," I said, "I was just going to ask you about the titles."

Later on I opened a bottle of port and we sat talking. While we were on our second glass Roeder arrived. Roeder is a friend of mine and a painter of the modern school, from whom I had bought a picture a few days earlier. His visit came at an awkward time, because for some reason or other I had not yet gotten around to hanging his picture. And now the two large landscapes were hanging on the wall instead.

After he had greeted us he went up to the two fateful pictures, and in a voice that expressed amazement mingled with disbelief he said: "Well, how about that! *Alpenglow* and *Before the Storm.*" "That's right," said my uncle, who was obviously surprised, "that's what they're actually called." I explained to Roeder that the pictures had just been given to me by my uncle, and as I spoke I tried to give him a meaningful look. But none of this seemed to make any impression on him: he just kept on muttering the words "Very nice, very nice," while his face wore a kind of distant expression. I had the feeling that villainous thoughts were at work behind that faraway look of his. I found his whole manner extremely tactless, and was glad when he took his leave shortly afterward. As we stood by the door he gave me a friendly tap on the shoulder—which was also quite unlike him. I started to feel distinctly uneasy, and for the rest of the evening I could feel the weight of his hand on my shoulder.

For his part my uncle stayed until the bottle was empty. When he left I breathed a sigh of relief: now I could take down the two pictures and hang Roeder's abstract on the wall instead. But all at once I was overcome by a feeling of disinclination, a curious sense of numbness. It might have been the aftereffects of the visit, or perhaps I was feeling tired after the wine. Port has that effect on one. Whatever the reason, the effort involved in climbing the step-ladder and changing the pictures suddenly seemed enormous. I decided to leave it.

Next morning a large crate was delivered to my flat. I'd just fetched my tools in readiness for changing over the pictures, so now I used them to open the crate instead. The first thing I found inside was a letter. It was from Roeder, and read as follows:

Dear Robert,

Enclosed you will find one or two things which I imagine should appeal to your taste.

Yours sincerely,
Roeder

Fearing the worst I set to work to unpack the crate. The first item was a porcelain flower vase wrapped up in excelsior; it was fashioned to look like a crane with brightly colored plumage, and its beak was open wide to receive the stems of the flowers. Next to this, swathed in layers of tissue paper, were a bunch of artificial roses and a table lamp in the shape of a naked female figure made out of cast iron, who supported on her shoulder a lampholder and a wire-framed lampshade covered in green silk, complete with ruffles and pleats.

When I saw these objects my mood darkened. Not that their arrival tempted me to suppose that Roeder really believed in some dramatic change in my tastes; but I did feel that he had gone too far with this childishly mischievous and deliberate "misunderstanding." Where on earth was I going to put these things in my two-room flat? I didn't have an attic or a boxroom.

I was still brooding on the tactlessness of this joke when Sylvia arrived. Sylvia is impulsive by nature, and always tends to follow her spontaneous inclinations without reserve. She often goes too far on these occasions—which is what happened now. Her quick eye must have taken in the situation at a glance. But instead of lending me moral support she behaved as if the difficulty consisted simply in deciding how to display a few new acquisitions to the best advantage. Without saying a word she went into action. She took a lightbulb from a drawer and screwed it into the lamp, which she then carried into my bedroom. Then she arranged the artificial flowers in the vase with a woman's fond care, put them on a shelf between the pictures, took a couple of paces backward, and observed the effect. Then she sat down next to me and stroked my cheek.

I turned toward her with a gesture of irritation. "Look here, Sylvia," I said, "this is all a terrible misunderstanding—in fact it's almost a conspiracy. Those pictures are a present from my uncle. He gave them to me last night. I should never have hung them up in the first place, but unfortunately I did. Then Roeder came and saw the pictures. And then . . ." At this point she interrupted me: "Why all the apologies? After all, what difference does it make how the things came into your possession? They belong to you now." The significance of these words was lost on me at the time, but the subsequent course of events was soon to make their meaning clearer. I sometimes fancy that what she actually said at the time was, "They belong *with* you now." At all events, that must have been what she meant.

When she left she said goodbye to me as one does to a patient whose hopes of recovery one is anxious not to undermine. She gazed straight into my eyes, as if she wanted to give me courage, stroked my cheek one more time, turned away abruptly, and was gone.

But she returned that same afternoon, bringing her friend Renate with her. Renate went straight to my bedroom and began hammering at something. Sylvia meanwhile unpacked a number of little lace covers, saying she would put them on the arms of the easy chairs straight away. They were sure to appeal to my taste—and anyway they protected the fabric of the upholstery. I was so indignant that I couldn't speak a word. I watched her, speechless, while she placed the lace covers on the arms of the chairs, smoothed them out, and fastened them with pins. Then she dragged me into the bedroom, where Renate had just finished hanging a large Black Forest cuckoo clock on the wall.

This was too much. In an access of frenzied rage I tried to rip the thing off the wall, but it was secured by two steel hooks; and as I was tugging at it the cuckoo shot out and uttered six loud shrieks right in my face. "Six o'clock already," said Renate, "we really must be going." As they took their leave—I was only dimly aware of the fact, being in something approaching a state of shock—Sylvia promised me she would embroider a few pretty tablecloths in cross-stitch for me. Then they both gave me a quick peck on the cheek and ran down the stairs, laughing as they went. I could still hear the sound of that laughter a long time after they had gone, as though an antagonist were laughing somewhere backstage after the curtain had already fallen.

The tablecloths done in cross-stitch arrived two days later. But that wasn't all. An architect friend of mine by the name of Mons had called round the evening before, saying that he'd heard about my new acquisitions from Roeder and had come round to have a look at them. I had tried to explain to him, in a state of nervous agitation which I made no attempt to conceal, that the whole thing was a ghastly mistake. But he had simply eyed me intently as I spoke, with the grave air of a diagnostician—as if he were trying to detect in my expression the further symptoms of some encroaching disease. This had made me even more agitated: and after he had pressed my hand as he was leaving, and said "Good night—old fellow," I was so furious that I hurled the door shut behind him.

The next day it arrived, accompanied by a card from him: a large, varnished, ivory-colored stand with shelves sticking out at various heights and angles. I knew at once that it was intended for displaying cactus plants. The plants themselves, in various shapes and sizes, were delivered later that same day, together with an illustrated booklet entitled *The Cactus Grower*. With a calmness that amazed me I arranged the cacti on the shelves and placed the booklet on my bedside table.

I had a restless night. The cuckoo woke me on several occasions. Each time I switched on the lamp my gaze fell upon the bronze female, and this was almost more than I could stand: so in order to take my mind off things I picked up *The Cactus Grower* from my bedside table. But I could not—as yet—summon up any enthusiasm for its contents, so I put the book down again and switched off the lamp. I was thinking unkind thoughts about my uncle, about Roeder, Sylvia and all the rest of them. But in the midst of such thoughts I did manage to drop off to sleep—until the cuckoo woke me up again.

Before the week was out I caught myself arranging the artificial flowers in the vase, or smoothing out one of the little lace covers on the arm of a chair; and when the crate containing the turned candlesticks and bowls was delivered I unpacked each item with eager interest. I didn't even notice who had sent them.

Then summer came. Sylvia had gone away, so the regular consignments of cross-stitch tablecloths and sofa cushions had now ceased. But she took to sending me color postcards instead, with views of various holiday beauty spots. I arranged the cards in an album.

Renate was still around, however, and one evening she brought me a boxed set of gramophone records. She wanted me to listen to a few pieces there and then, so we put on a fantasia entitled "Scenes from Weber's Magic Forest," followed by "Highlights from Wagner's Operas," and ending up with the finale of Beethoven's Fifth Symphony. Then she left. When she had gone I put on the ballet music from *Rosamunde* and listened to that, then went to bed. The cuckoo clock struck twelve. I was getting used to it—in fact I was coming to rely on it.

There was one more occasion when I tried to rebel. It was the day that Herr von Stamitz, who by now was engaged to Sylvia, sent me the bookcase in decorated walnut together with the dummy sets of books. I really can't think why I should have worked myself up into such an uncontrollable fury on this particular occasion; as a piece of craftsmanship there was not a single fault to find with the thing. But I remember how I ran around the flat like a caged animal. I tried to snatch the lace covers off the easy chairs, forgetting that I had subsequently sewn them on. I would have ripped a few of the cross-stitch tablecloths apart with my teeth, but they were too tough, being made of good stout country linen. Sylvia had never been one to use inferior-quality materials. The only thing that did get broken in all this was a valuable piece of African sculpture—one of the few mementos of the period before my uncle's visit. I couldn't help laughing at the solemn irony of this accident; and my rage subsided. I calmly set to work to arrange the backs of the books in the walnut bookcase, securing them at both ends. As I worked my eye fell upon the names of Gibbon, Macaulay, Mommsen, and Ranke. It was a selection for historians. I might add that history has always been one of my interests.

That night I dreamed I was wandering through great empty chambers, with just the occasional piece of functional-looking furniture here and there. I sat down on a steel stool: and at once it sprouted an upholstered back and armrests, with cushions of velvet and rep. Crystal chandeliers were lowered from the ceiling. Women dressed in flowing robes, with their hair coiled into buns above their ears, wheeled in great gold-edged tomes and opened them before me. The pages were covered with engravings and photographs that had been stuck in, with captions like "Franz Liszt in the circle of his friends," "Eventide on the shores of the Walchensee," or "Hiroshima mon amour." I woke up just as the pendulum clock in the living room was striking three, switched on the lamp by my bed, and saw the bronze figure standing there before me, a hideously tangible presence. I switched off the lamp again, whereupon the cuckoo shrieked three times—the clock was obviously slow—so I switched on the lamp once more and hurled The Cactus Grower at the cuckoo, but missed, so I tried again with the Rosenthal china stag, but only succeeded in hitting a rather risqué engraving—"la surprise"—which was hanging next to the cuckoo clock. The glass shattered and I calmed down. The crisis was past.

And so my flat gradually became choked with things. The number of my visitors steadily decreased, since it was now becoming quite difficult to work one's way through the accumulated furniture to find a seat; and when visitors did manage to get through they couldn't sit down anyway, because the chairs were piled high with framed prints and pottery of every kind, including many a piece that had won an award for its elegantly functional design.

My uncle came to visit me one more time, but I didn't actually see him because I was in bed, and he couldn't find the way through to me. He had brought a picture with him—he called out to tell me that it was "something modern" this time—and so I asked him to leave it on one of the teak occasional tables of which there were no doubt several in the hall. He called out to say that the occasional tables were already filled with all kinds of ceramic pots—obviously items of considerable artistic value. I didn't bother to reply, and I don't know whether my uncle left the picture or took it away again, because ever since then I've stayed in bed. My uncle was the last visitor I had.

I don't get out of bed anymore, because even though I can find my way through the bedroom I get lost in the living room. So I just lie in bed and doze, look at postcards or photogravures, or play records on the gramophone next to my bed—Schubert's "Serenade," or the "Ave Maria" sung by a Negro singer. She has such a lovely soothing voice. And from time to time I dip into *The Cactus Grower*, from which I have learned, for instance, that cacti sometimes flower. Perhaps one of mine is flowering now and I don't know it: as I said, I don't visit my living room anymore.

I'm able to sleep again now, having managed to get the cuckoo one night just as he was about to slip back inside—I landed a direct hit with a Swedish glass vase. The pendulum clock in the living room stopped a long time ago, and I can't get to it any more to wind it up. Not that I would want to, anyway: what would be the point?

NOTES ON CONTRIBUTORS

JOHN ALLMAN is an associate professor at Rockland Community College in Suffern, New York. His book, *Walking Four Ways in the Wind,* was published in the fall of 1979 by Princeton University Press in the Princeton Series of Contemporary Poets. He is currently working on a new collection, *Dostoevsky at Semyonov Square,* based on historical subjects, 1849–1948.

HORST BIENEK was born in 1930 in Gleiwitz, Upper Silesia, in what is now Poland. After having been released from a Soviet labor camp in 1956, he became a West German citizen and now resides in Munich. A poet, essayist, and fiction writer, Bienek attracted attention with his experimental novels *The Cell* (1968) and *Bakunin: An Invention* (1970). Popular as well as critical acclaim has greeted his two recent novels, *The First Polka* (1975) and *September Light* (1977), which also won him the prestigious Wilhelm Raabe Award. RALPH READ is an associate professor of German at the University of Texas at Austin.

For information on MIHAIL CHEMIAKIN, see the introduction to his "Ten Drawings."

ANNALISA CIMA lives in Milan, where she is an editor at the firm of Saggiatore. She has published a number of books of poetry, including *Sesamon, Immobilità,* and *Terzo Modo,* from which the selection in these pages was translated. SIZZO DE RACHEWILTZ lives in Merano, Italy, and is now writing a dissertation on the Siren in literature. MARY DE RACHEWILTZ is the author of *Ezra Pound, Father and Teacher: Discretions* (New Directions, 1975).

Among the many translated volumes of the work of JEAN COCTEAU (1889–1963), New Directions publishes *The Holy Terrors* and *The Infernal Machine & Other Plays.* CHARLES GUENTHER is the author of *Phrase/Paraphrase* (poems), brought out by The Prairie Press, Iowa City, in 1970. A translator, poet, and critic, he lives in St. Louis.

Doug Crowell has been working on a novel about Billy the Kid. His fiction has been published in *Epoch, Buffalo Spree, New Writers,* and *Fiction Texas,* among other magazines.

Last year, New Directions brought out *Robert Duncan: Scales of the Marvelous,* an exploration of Robert Duncan's poetry, edited by Robert J. Bertholf and Ian W. Reid. Duncan's *Fictive Certainties: Five Essays in Essential Autobiography* is now in preparation.

Lawrence Ferlinghetti's "The White Newsy" is a companion piece to "An Elegy to Dispel Gloom," included in the San Francisco poet's most recent collection, *Landscapes of Living & Dying.*

Some of David Giannini's poems appeared in *ND23* and *ND26.* He is the author of several books, most recently *Close Packet* (Jays Hill Press, 1978), and was poet-in-residence in 1977–78 for the Williamstown (Massachusetts) Public Schools.

Sidney Goldfarb's books of poetry include *Speech, for Instance* (1969) and *Messages* (1971), both published by Farrar, Straus & Giroux, and just recently *Curve in the Road,* brought out by Halty Ferguson.

For information on William Heinesen, see the translator's note preceding his story "The Night of the Gryla." Hedin Bronner has taught at American universities and at the University of Oslo. His numerous books and articles on Scandinavian literature include a forthcoming volume of short stories by Heinesen, translated into English and entitled *The Man from Malta and Other Stories.*

Wolfgang Hildesheimer is a young German writer best known for his book *Zeiten in Cornwall* (Suhrkamp), of which an excerpt has appeared in *Dimension,* the magazine of German literature published at the University of Texas. "Finding My Way" is from his collection of stories *Lieblose Legenden* (Suhrkamp). Allan Blunden is a free-lance translator, specializing in German, who lives in the village of Liskeard in Cornwall.

Brett Masseaux was born in Philadelphia in 1954. Along with his "Fright Fables," he has written several one-act plays, humorous works, and newspaper articles. "The Score Sheet" is his first published fiction.

For information on CARLOS NEJAR, see the introduction to his "Eight Poems." GIOVANNI PONTIERO teaches in the Department of Spanish and Portuguese Studies at the University of Manchester. His translations of contemporary Brazilian literature have appeared in *ND37* and *ND39*.

NICANOR PARRA is one of Chile's leading poets. Two bilingual collections of his work, *Poems and Antipoems* (1967) and *Emergency Poems* (1972), are published by New Directions. STEVEN WHITE spent several months last year on a coffee farm in Nicaragua and recently finished translating an anthology of Nicaraguan poetry.

TOBY OLSON's two most recent books of poetry are *Aesthetics* (Membrane Press, Milwaukee) and *The Florence Poems* (Permanent Press, London). New Directions published his novel, *The Life of Jesus*, in 1976. His new novel, "Seaview," is now close to completion.

This year, Viking/Penguin Publishers is bringing out a clothbound edition of three of JAMES PURDY's works—*Malcolm, The Nephew*, and the long story *63: Dream Palace*—under the general title of *Dream Palace*. His short fiction, poetry, and plays appear regularly in these pages.

Curator of Russian and East European Studies at Yale, ALEKSIS RANNIT is one of the foremost poets in the Estonian language. "The Violin of Monsieur Ingres," a selection of his first assays in English, is reproduced from his own elegant hand.

JEROME ROTHENBERG's newest book is *Vienna Blood & Other Poems*. His other collections with New Directions are *A Seneca Journal* (1978), *Poems from the Game of Silence* (1975), and *Poland/1931* (1974).

GUSTAF SOBIN's work has appeared most recently in *Montemora, Ironwood, Kayak*, and *Text*. A book of his poems, *Mirrorhead*, was brought out last year by the Montemora Foundation.

For information on PATIENCE WORTH, see the note preceding her "Selected Poems." STEPHEN BRAUDE, who gathered and transcribed the material here, teaches philosophy at the University of Maryland, Baltimore County. He is the author of *ESP & PK: A Philosophical Examination* (1979).